THE
MIDNIGHT
LULLABY

THE
MIDNIGHT
LULLABY

CHERYL LOW

A

Grinning Skull Press

Publication

PO Box 67, Bridgewater, MA 02324

DEDICATION

To my partner in all things. All love stories are tragedies. Every great romance has a horror waiting at the end. But even knowing that, I wouldn't want my story to go any differently.

Acknowledgments

A huge thank you to Grinning Skull Press for taking on another of my books and for being so fantastic to work with!

CHAPTER ONE

Benedict was eight years old, sitting on a stiff chair in the dark hallway of a house he didn't know. He clamped his hands around the edges of his seat, trying to press his bones so tight that they wouldn't shake. His head whipped from side to side, unblinking as he searched for shapes.

"Tell me where it is!" Gloria's voice boomed from the room down the hall. Benedict winced, squinting to see through the doorway and into the wild flicker of candle-light.

The witch screamed, writhing on the floor at Gloria's feet. She chanted between her howls, head thumping back against the floor and narrow chest pushing high. Even from this distance, and even with her screeches in the air, he heard her bones cracking.

"Give me the book!" Gloria roared.

Wind rushed through the house, knocking the pictures from the walls. Windows cracked in their frames. Doors opened and closed with furious bangs upstairs.

"Can you see them?" Elysium whispered.

Benedict gulped ragged breaths, fear marching a parade through his chest with the big drums in his ears. "No."

His brother sighed, the teen crouching in front of Benedict. "Benny, there." He pointed down the hall, toward the open doorway and their mother's booming voice demanding to know where the spirit-wielder hid her book of secrets. "*There*. You see that one? He's big. You have to see him."

Benedict cried but didn't blink at the tears, staring down the hall through a liquid haze. He saw the doorway and the lights inside and his mother's shadow cast across the twisting woman on the floor. "There's no one in the hall," he confessed.

The floorboards squeaked; he saw them straining and heard the heavy footfalls coming toward them, but he didn't see the ghost.

"What's happening?" Benedict begged, small voice almost lost under the raging of the house. He jumped at a scratching sound, claws on hardwood, and a sickly meowing.

"The witch is calling the spirits she's trapped here," his brother explained.

"Will they hurt Mother?" Benedict asked, still staring down the hallway. The heavy steps getting closer.

"Do you see him yet?" Elysium asked rather than answering, head whipping back and forth, watching something in the empty hall and studying his baby brother.

Benedict wrinkled his nose, trying not to cry.

The floorboards creaked closer and closer, his little heart fluttering wildly in his chest.

"Benny, you see him, right?" Elysium shouted over the groaning walls and wailing woman—over the scratching and the creaking and that awful meowing. "Benny—"

Benedict screamed when something pulled Elysium away from him and dragged his older brother down the hall, tossing him into a dark parlor with a heavy thud.

Benedict jumped down from his chair and ran after him, tears spilling over his lashes. He didn't see whatever they saw, but he knew it was real. He looked around at the empty chairs and couches, his hands balled into fists against his sides. "Elysium?" he whispered.

A thump on the wall drew his gaze up, eyes straining and vision blurring at the edges.

His brother was there, pinned against the wall by an unseen force and held so high up that the top of his head almost brushed the ceiling. Elysium rasped in ragged breaths, heels kicking against the wall.

Benedict backed up, unable to look away until he bumped into a closet door. The scratching grew louder, the yowling from inside desperate. He twisted around and stared at the doorknob.

He knew he shouldn't open it, but a whisper told him he

had to. Something was inside…something that needed out.

The boy reached up and used both hands to turn the knob. The door opened with a pop, and he shuffled back from it. For one blessed moment, the scratching stopped, the meowing went silent, and then the mangy monsters poured out. Cats, twisted and thin, half-decayed but still moving. Their claws scratched against the floor, never retracting into their paws, some with no meat to call a paw anymore. One looked up at Benedict, an empty socket and the glint of bone flashing at him. It meowed, and he could see the vocal cords rattling in its neck where the fur and flesh were missing.

He screamed, but the house only grew louder, trying to smother him.

And then he was off his feet.

For a second, he choked on his sounds, terrified that the ghost had snatched him up like it had Elysium, and then he inhaled and knew exactly whose arms he was in. His brother held him against his shoulder and ran from the room, kicking the door shut behind them. He didn't stop, running straight down the corridor and toward the sound of their mother's voice. Benedict buried his face in that shoulder, rubbing his tears out in the fabric of his shirt and hoping even now that Mother wouldn't notice how he had cried.

Elysium put him down on his feet in a corner of the room, kneeling in front of him and pulling a piece of white chalk from his vest pocket. Benedict, drowning in his own fear, couldn't stop gasping for air. Elysium drew a half-circle on the wood floor from wall to wall, closing Benedict into the corner, and then started sketching runes over the edges of the circle. "Don't move," he yelled over the storm of spirits.

Benedict bit his lip to keep from whining, looking past Elysium at the woman writhing in the middle of the room. She clawed score marks into the floorboards like the cats had, her orange hair long and knotted around her face and shoulders. Her boots thudded and kicked, but she couldn't get away, pinned there on the ground by Gloria Lyon's will. His mother stood over her, her dark hair braided over one shoulder and her sharp, black suit making her look like a shadow come to life. "Relent the book. Release the spirits. And I will spare you," Gloria shouted, unmoved by all the shows of power the other woman had displayed—by all the fury of her creations in this house.

The woman on the floor screamed, and Benedict could hear windows breaking.

Elysium cupped the sides of his face in his hands, making Benedict look at him rather than them. "Okay, Benny. You know how this works."

Benedict swallowed hard, trying again not to cry. He nodded once, and Elysium flashed him a smile.

Benedict closed his eyes.

The battle of wills continued to rage on, screams and thuds rampant in the house, but he didn't open his eyes to see. He pressed the heels of his palms into his ears when the screaming grew to be too much, shaking his head when he heard Elysium cry out in pain and gasping for air when those horrible yowls grew closer and closer.

But he didn't open his eyes. Not until the house had finally gone quiet hours later. Not until his mother picked him up from the corner and carried him out of the house. She put him in the back seat of the car, and he waited. When she came back, Elysium was with her, one arm broken and folded to his chest and the other carrying a worn, leather-bound notebook.

Benedict blinked out the window. The sun peeked over the houses down the hillside in bright wisps of pink and orange. When the house they had come from went up in flames, it wasn't wisps of orange like the ones in the sky. There were no shades of pink. Just violent, furious heat.

Gloria had not spared the woman inside—not even when she gave up her book and released the spirits she had bound to her home.

Even Benedict, at eight years old, had known she wouldn't show mercy. It wasn't her way.

Chapter Two

Twenty Years Later

Benedict circled the room, inspecting a fireplace almost as high as he was tall. He scrutinized the matching ceramic vases on either side, the white chesterfield sofa and chairs arranged around a marble coffee table, and finally, the massive gilded mirror dominating one wall. The home, recently purchased, was impeccably furnished for the design of the estate without giving up the antique feeling this place oozed. Benedict Lyon liked it. He could see himself living here, if it weren't haunted.

"*It's a bit much,*" Emmeline commented, as though hearing his thoughts, which she *could not* do. In his life, he'd met just about every spiritualist there was and never found one that could really read thoughts, though he had had the pleasure of meeting a few mentalists who had certainly made it look like they could.

Benedict ignored her remark and paused in his inspection of the house to give himself a once-over in the gilded mirror. He ghosted fingers across the black wave of his hair, swept up and sprayed into place, back from his face. He had been told his wide, red mouth had a lustful quality; he didn't see it himself, but he liked knowing it was there. His vest hugged his waist, creating the cut of a silhouette he chased with unhindered vanity. His family had never been inclined to fear sins, only what they left behind on the world. As long as he knew himself well enough to see those flaws, neither his vanity nor his pride would bring him down.

Emmeline coughed, a forced sound to remind him that he was on the clock and not at home.

He spun away from the mirror and considered the room as a whole. He had made a show of studying the last four rooms on the first floor with the same intensity.

Mr. Whittle followed him closely but stayed breathlessly quiet, no more than a whisper of silk trailing him through the house. The man, well into his fifties but fit enough to shame most thirty-year-olds, had called through his network of associations and friends to reach out to the Lyons—a family known for being gifted. Benedict had giggled at that term as a boy, and he still did sometimes, when no one was around to notice. Mr. Whittle and his husband had been hoping for Benedict's eldest brother, Elysium, or even his cousin, Theodore, who had become a flashy medium with his own TV special. Instead, they got Benedict, the runt of the illustrious ghost-hunting family.

Luckily, no one, including Mr. Whittle, had any idea

just how much of a psychic dullard Benedict was.

Emmeline groaned, twirling in frustration near the door. She got bored easily. "*There's nothing in here but tacky furniture!*"

Benedict flashed her a frown. He liked the furniture.

Emmeline's dress fluttered around her thighs, falling back into place when she stopped spinning. The blue cotton ballooned out at her hips, creating a bell-shape that accentuated the narrowest part of her body just under her bust. She was far from a slim girl, that bell of skirt full of hips and thighs. Her dark hair was in a messy tie, always caught in the moment before it fell to obscure her heart-shaped face.

"There is definitely a presence here," Benedict said solemnly, countering her outburst of boredom. He turned toward Mr. Whittle.

The man held his hands to his chest, clutching at an invisible lump. "We had to move the kids back to the house in the city," he complained. "It was just a few sounds and things disappearing at first."

Emmeline rolled her eyes and spun away from the room, turning up the staircase and stomping away on bare feet. "*If you have a house in the city, then move back to it!*" she shouted before grumbling, "*Rich people...*"

Mr. Whittle let out a groan of distress, sliding closer to Benedict. "Please, your brother said you'd be able to clean the house—"

"*Cleanse,*" Benedict corrected quickly, not liking the sound of cleaning any house that wasn't his own. "I can sense something amiss, but there doesn't seem to be anything rooted in these rooms. May we continue upstairs?"

"Of course. Please." Mr. Whittle nodded eagerly and led the way to the second floor. "We were planning to do a remodel. Do you think that could have caused the unrest?"

Benedict smiled gently. "From the beautiful state of your home, I suspect you did a bit of remodeling when you moved in."

Mr. Whittle flashed a pleased grin, proud of his home.

"I doubt the spirit minds then. It's not like you're planning to knock the house down, are you?"

"No, no. Nothing like that."

They reached the second-floor landing, and Mr. Whittle opened the first door to the right and disappeared inside. "This is my daughter's room."

Benedict stopped before he reached it, staring straight down the hallway to the very end.

Emmeline stood there, staring up a narrow staircase. She seemed frozen, stalk-still and holding her breath.

Mr. Whittle poked his head back out of the bedroom. "Mister Lyon?"

Benedict ignored him, taking measured steps toward her. Her lips moved, the faintest of whispers rushing out. He could nearly make out her words, the flood of them so hurried, almost hissing. Her head snapped to the side, gaze locking with Benedict's, and he jerked to a stop.

"What's up there?" he asked.

"A playroom for the kids," Mr. Whittle replied. "Haven't really used it in years, not since they outgrew it. We're planning to turn it into a guest apartment."

Benedict continued to hold Emmeline's gaze. She was unreadable, with too many emotions beyond the understanding of the living. She turned away as though drawn from him in a trance and went up the stairs. Benedict's stomach dropped, certain that something awful would happen as soon as she was out of sight.

He knew he was frightening Mr. Whittle now, but he couldn't wait to explain. He hurried after her with the older man on his heels.

Benedict took the stairs two at a time and came up in the attic playroom. It was bright, lit from the half-circle windows dominating the triangular wall on the far side. A bright blue rug spread across the white-painted wood floor while mirrors and pictures dressed the walls. A comfortable couch sat to the left and little play furniture had been pushed to the far end of the room. A large chest of toys and a stack of board games were arranged in the corner. It was the sort of messy that looked designed, ready for a photoshoot.

"*There's a child's ghost here,*" Emmeline said quietly, staring at the corner with the games and toys. "*He likes this room the way it is but misses the other kids.*" Her fingers curled slightly, and Benedict realized she was holding the spirit's hand, pressed into the side of her skirts as though to hide it from him. She does that sometimes, hides ghosts from him. She told him once that not all spirits were harmful, that they're just not ready to go and need a little more time. She didn't like the idea of them being pushed out and would rather he leave them to walk about the place between worlds until they faded on their own.

"*He died in the woods outside. He got lost and couldn't find his way home. He was happy when he saw the other kids playing and followed them back here. He says he didn't do any of the bad things in the house.*" She paused then, a shadow of worry crossing her features when she looked down at the apparition at her side.

Benedict couldn't see it. Only her.

"*The boy says there is a…scary man.*"

Benedict pressed his lips. That sounded promising for the job but unpleasant for his own sanity.

He swayed on his feet, eyes fluttering shut and hand going to his temple. Mr. Whittle jumped closer, catching Benedict's elbow to steady him. "Are you okay, Mister Lyon?"

Benedict took an exaggerated swallow of air and steadied himself, pressing a hand to his chest. "You have a little spirit here, in this room with us now…"

Mr. Whittle sucked a breath and turned, looking about as though he might spot it. His fingers pressed tighter on Benedict's arm.

"A child," Benedict went on, gasping and opening his eyes. They were teary. He could cry on command. He had mastered that little talent years ago to help sell the experience. "He's young, and he means you no harm. A tragic soul. He was lost in the woods, died there, and continued to search for a way home—unaware of his own state. He was alone for so long, searching for the warmth of home, until one day he heard the laughter of your children playing. He followed the sound from those dark, lonely woods and came here." He turned toward Mr. Whittle, catching his hand when it left his sleeve. "Your family has given him such a sense of peace and safety," he said, peering deep into the older man's eyes and seeing that fear and pity blossom into pride. "He'll move on soon. He's so grateful to you for letting him be here. For letting him come home."

Benedict gave himself chills with that line, and Mr. Whittle's eyes filled with tears. "Oh," was all he managed before rallying a question. "What's his name?"

"*George*," Emmeline prompted.

"George," Benedict repeated with soft reverence. "And he promises that he hasn't been responsible for the loud sounds and broken things." Benedict paused, pretending to listen and laugh gently at something sweet the boy said. "He says he's a good boy and would never mess up the house."

Emmeline rolled her eyes at him; he knew without even looking.

"Oh," Mr. Whittle said again, eyes big and clear now, holding tight to Benedict's hand. "Then what is causing it?" he whispered, as though the culprit might overhear him.

"*It's another spirit*," Emmeline answered.

Benedict glanced in her direction. She wasn't standing off to the side with the forgotten piles of toys anymore. She was at the windows, chin down and gaze fixed outside.

"There is something else here…" Benedict said, gently moving away from Mr. Whittle and toward the window. He stood beside her, looking past her and out at the lawn sloping off the back of the property. It led down to a large creek with a little dock and thick woods on the other side. A rowboat tied to the dock bobbed gently in the shade of a shed at the very edge of the bank.

"*He's out there,*" Emmeline said, her voice distant. He wished he could take her hand just to make sure she really was with him still. But she was never *really* with him, not like that. His Emmeline was dead. He had never held her hand and never would.

"I see him," Benedict lied.

"*He's big and soaking wet,*" Emmeline continued. "*He's wearing a heavy jacket, and his breath forms in the air, like it's cold…*"

It was July. It was far from cold out.

"*There's ice stuck to his jacket and his overalls,*" Emmeline said.

"The creek," Benedict spoke, dragging his words out as though they were being tugged from his body unwillingly. He swayed in the mimic of a trance. "It was frozen. There is a presence in your home… *A man…* He brings the cold inside with him. He is soaked to the bone, dripping water and slush from the winter he can never escape."

Mr. Whittle gasped. "There have been wet footprints down the halls! Sometimes with clumps of snow, like it was tracked into the house, but it's not even winter."

"Yes," Benedict confirmed, creasing his brow and faking a pained headache—contact with spirits can do that, or so he heard.

"*He's looking back at me,*" Emmeline whispered be-side him, and his eyes snapped open to stare at the spot out-side where her gaze had fixed. He saw nothing, of course. Benedict never felt more like a charlatan than in these moments, when everything was working. He had the homeowner convinced. It wasn't a complete lie, though, because the ghosts were real. They were there. He just couldn't see them.

"*He knows we're here,*" Emmeline said and then took a step back, away from the window. "*Someone struck him over the head when he was cutting wood… They dragged him to the river. Used the ax to break the ice and pushed him in.*"

"Mister Whittle, I think you do have a problem here," Benedict confessed, turning toward the man. His breath formed in the air, the room suddenly frigid cold as though they stood in a meat-locker rather than a playroom.

Mr. Whittle curled his arms around himself instinctively. "Oh, this happens sometimes…" he said. "We had someone out to check the AC, but—"

"It's not that," Benedict confirmed.

"*He's here,*" Emmeline said, voice deadpan.

Benedict turned toward her and the window, startled to find her staring back at him.

"*He wants them to leave. He wants to be alone.*" Dangerous levels of understanding weighed heavily in her voice. Ghosts had an almost inescapable nature that drew them into their own anger and the anger of others. They didn't feed on it so much as their anger consumed them. He saw it in Emmeline sometimes, making her dark eyes flicker with shades of vivid green.

Benedict parted his lips but forgot his words when her gaze slipped from his, staring past him—and up, at someone very tall.

For the flash of a second, she almost looked frightened, and then her nerves stilled, her shoulders pressing back and her chin high. Benedict took one step closer to her, slid to the side, and peered into her eyes until he saw the reflection of the room like a shadow laid over her irises. There was Mr. Whittle, wringing his wrists and standing beside the lumpy shape of the couch. Her eyes widened a little, unblinking and fixed on the room. A large, dark figure took a step forward. Benedict heard that heavy boot on the floor, and from the sound Mr. Whittle made, so did he.

A dragging sound scraped across his nerves, clawing up his spine. The hulking silhouette reflected in her eye lifted an ax from the floor, tossed it back over a shoulder, and then lurched toward Mr. Whittle.

Chapter Three

Benedict swore beneath his breath and twisted away from Emmeline. His shoes caught the edge of the rug when he launched himself at Mr. Whittle, almost tripping and jerking the coffee table. He tackled the man, pushing a startled breath from Mr. Whittle's lungs before they both landed heavily onto the floor between the couch and the low table.

"What on—" Mr. Whittle had only just begun to protest when the table beside them was cleaved in half with a thunderous crack.

Benedict collected himself quickly and was on his feet with both hands gripping the front of the other man's jacket, hauling him up and pushing him back into the nearest corner. A distorted roar burst through the room, shaking the walls and battering their senses. Benedict pressed Mr. Whittle into the corner, holding him there until he knew to stay put. Benedict stepped back, plunging his hands into the pockets of his slacks. His left came up with a stub of chalk. He crouched down and drew a half-circle, encasing Mr. Whittle in the corner, and quickly scraped little figures into the edges of the line, mouthing old words his mother had taught him.

"Ben..." Emmeline said his name somewhere in the storm still raging through the room, rattling the pictures off the walls and shaking the floorboards underfoot.

Benedict thumbed open a pocketknife in his right hand, sliced the pad of his thumb, and dropped blood onto the newly etched seal. "Close your eyes," he ordered Mr. Whittle as he stood. "If you don't look, it won't see you." A flimsy patch for a leaking boat; no one could keep their eyes closed forever. His brother had done this to him once, hidden him from a spirit while they finished the job. Of course, he had been a child at the time. They had dragged him along in hopes that the danger of the situation would bring his gifts to birth. It hadn't worked, though he had been given enough material to fuel his nightmares for life and a thorough understanding that there were plenty of things in the world he could not see—and that *did not* make them any less real.

"Benedict!" Emmeline shouted.

He turned to see her standing much closer, eyes big and gaze cutting between him and something between them. Oh God, it was right there? Right in front of him? He rolled the piece of chalk between his fingers, thoughtlessly wetting it with his blood. All at once, the room stilled, and not in a calm-at-the-end-of-a-storm sort of way, but frozen, caught in a second that held fast. And then the frames of the pictures on the floor burst, the walls cracked, and Benedict was lifted off his feet. He hated being lifted by spirits. It wasn't the sense of hands jerking him upward. It wasn't a pull on his clothing or a grip on his arm. It was pressure everywhere, seizing up his body and dragging him into the air as though gravity had abandoned him.

He couldn't breathe; his only comfort was in knowing that it wouldn't last. It never did. It took too much energy to lift someone. Not even the most powerful poltergeists could hold a person long enough to smother them though they had plenty of other ways of doing damage.

Gravity returned to him. His body hurtled through the air, across the room, and slammed shoulder-first into the half-circle of windows. They shattered, and daylight blinded him. An embarrassing "*hmph*" escaped his lips when he tumbled out the window and rolled down the slant of the roof.

He landed on his back in a thick bed of peonies, blooms bursting with white and pink petals all around him. For a long, dizzy second, he lay there, staring up at the bright, blue sky. At least it hadn't been a rose bed. He sat up, shaky hands patting himself in search of broken bones. None. He stood, grabbing hold of an iron fence to steady himself before noticing the spikes at the top that could have easily impaled him if he had been a couple of inches to the left. He gagged a little, almost losing his lunch.

"What are you doing?" Emmeline yelled.

He looked up at the broken window, expecting her to be leaning out it.

"Get your shit together!" she snapped, and he jumped, finding her standing on the other side of the fence. She passed through it when she closed in on him. *"He knows why you're here."*

Benedict groaned. That was the problem with his ghost partner—if she saw into other spirits, they could see just as well into her.

"Where?" he grunted the question.

Her arm stretched out, pointing toward the creek and the little shed at the back of the property.

Benedict nodded, head throbbing when he did. He started dragging himself in that direction. His back twinged, his legs stiff, but every step got easier, faster, under the mounting sense of urgency.

The slope of the grass helped, downhill always better than uphill. He sank his hand into his pocket again, fishing out another bit of chalk. He couldn't remember dropping the last piece, somewhere between being picked up by a ghost and tossed out a window. Luckily, he always carried extra.

"He's coming," Emmeline said, suddenly beside him, keeping pace and throwing quick glances back toward the house.

Benedict almost lost his step when he reached the shed beside the narrow dock. He ground his teeth against the sharp pain shooting up his back. Sunlight glittered off the clear stream as it rolled over the stones, darkening under the shadow of the dock. He shouldered open the flimsy door and fell inside. Dust billowed up from the old wood planks. Crates of lawn decorations, fishing rods and supplies, and gardening tools gathered in the corners. He couldn't help but notice the ax leaning against the wall, cobwebs collected around it as though binding it to the spot. Falling to his knees, Benedict swept his arms across the floor to push the stacks of junk aside, clearing a spot. He touched the chalk down, barely starting to draw the seal when a furious, booming voice made his stomach drop.

"What's his name?" Benedict shouted.

"Roger Clifton James," Emmeline answered, voice steady but outside the shed.

He wrote the name inside the seal, looked over his work once, and then nodded, crawling to his feet and reaching for the old ax. His fingers brushed the rough wood wall, the corner, cobwebs, but not the handle of the ax. He twisted toward it, staring at the empty spot before turning a full circle to study the little shed. The ax was gone.

The roaring of the ghost had ended, nothing but the gentle rush of the creek and the groaning of floorboards underfoot.

Catching his breath, Benedict slowly opened the shed door. The ax lay on the soft, grassy bank of the stream. He took a step outside, gaze sliding up to where Emmeline stood not far beyond the weapon. She leaned up on her toes, toward nothing he could see. She spoke softly. Had she calmed the ghost? Soothed Mr. James into a trance of some kind?

Benedict took long, careful strides toward the ax, as though being quiet would allow him to go undetected.

He could make out the soft sound of Emmeline's voice, rushed, as though the words she spoke were coming out piled on top of one another, no spaces in between. He was almost to the ax when he chanced another glance up at her. Her eyes shone a vivid green, brighter than any blade of grass or perfectly lit emerald. The corners of her mouth grew sharp, teeth clicking every so often around her hushed words. It couldn't be calming, whatever she said to the ghost. It just couldn't be.

He didn't have the time to worry about it or second guess his choices. He needed to get the ax and break the seal in the shed. He needed—

His breath came out in a cold cloud just as he touched the handle of the ax. He stared down, the grass gone and his fingers curling into snow to wrap around the handle. That wasn't possible. This spirit couldn't be strong enough to make him see something like this, to feel the dry cold of the snow clinging to his skin.

Benedict had only begun to straighten his legs and stand when a body slammed into his, lifting him up and pushing him back. Together, he and the ghost crashed into the water. He felt it break under his back, not the way water should break, but the way thin ice might. Cold enveloped his body, but he felt it most around his skull and down his spine, agony slicing through him with such a shock that he bowed, arching into the other man. He was pushed down until his back touched the stones at the bottom. He tried to get to the surface, but a weight held him down.

He forced his eyes open, cold stinging at every nerve. The blue water shimmered with shapes of the world beyond the surface, bright with all the white outlines of winter. The surface was so close. He reached up, his fingers pushing out of the water, chunks of ice bumping his knuckles.

She stood there at the water's edge, looking back at him. For one terrible second, Benedict stilled, staring at Emmeline. Her mouth opened, gasping for air, and tears slid from her green eyes. Misery pooled in her expression, swirling in all the details of it. He saw everything in her then, splayed out before him. She was frightened, heartbroken, furious, and unsure. But what she wasn't was merciful.

What had she done?

Why?

Had the anger of the other ghost infected her?

How could she look at him like that? Like she was frightened to see him die but eager for it at the same time. What had he done to deserve it? Was she caught up in her own ghostly anger and lashing out? Would she regret it? No. No, he couldn't see anything about her now that would let him imagine regret in her later.

Suddenly Benedict gulped air—warm, summer air. He blinked, shaking and shivering, his teeth clattering and arms stiff with cold when he curled them around his chest. Mr. Whittle stood in front of him, ankle-deep in the creek and holding him up with a grip on either arm. Shards of ice fell off Benedict's shirt and vest, melting quickly in the July heat.

Benedict, still shaking with the cold that had pierced his bones, dragged himself up the bank. He reached out for the ax, hand trembling and fingers blue. Mr. Whittle grabbed it quickly up off the grass and handed it to him.

Emmeline stood off to the side, staring anywhere but at him and not looking particularly apologetic either.

Benedict walked past her, into the shed, and hacked at the floor with the old ax, cracking the floorboards and the seal, chopping Mr. Roger Clifton James's name into pieces.

Almost as soon as it was done, the cold released his bones. He waited a moment in the quiet that followed, listening to the creek outside. This was the moment where one of his siblings or cousins would extend their supernatural senses out into the world around them and see if the angry ghost was still present. Benedict could not do that, so he pretended. But he was sure Mr. Roger Clifton James was gone—because he had done this dozens of times before and they were always gone when he and Emmeline left.

Benedict walked out of the shed, handed Mr. Whittle

the ax, and informed him that the violent spirit was gone—purged from the family house. He assured him it would not return. They never did once they had been sent on.

Mr. Whittle barely knew what to say, flabbergasted as he gripped the ax.

Benedict shook the man's hand and thanked him for saving his life in much the same manner he might thank a person for a good cup of coffee. Nonetheless, Mr. Whittle inflated with pride and held the ax a bit more confidently.

"Would you like me to call you a doctor, Mister Lyon? You're soaked to the bone. We must get you dried off and—"

"Not necessary, sir," Benedict assured him, starting up the grassy slope toward the house. He wasn't moving as quickly now, and the angle of the ground was no longer in his favor. "It is a long drive, and I really would like to get home to rest." He played up his spiritual exhaustion for the man, as though falling out a window wasn't enough to account for his hobbling stride.

Mr. Whittle persisted until Benedict made up some bit about needing to leave the house quickly so that it could settle back into its natural state without the magnet of his *extraordinary* spirit in the way.

He unbuttoned and peeled off his wet jacket, socks squishing inside his shoes as he marched across the gravel driveway to his car. He unbuttoned his vest, peeling it off, too, and throwing both garments into the backseat. Emmeline stood on the other side of the car, and for a moment, he stood there, their eyes locked.

Her jaw was set, her lips pressed, and her chin ever so slightly upturned. There was no apology in her gaze.

Benedict took a deep breath and settled into the driver's seat, drenched to the bone and puddling on the leather seat.

He glanced in the rearview mirror. Emmeline sat in the corner of the backseat, arms folded, and attention turned out the window. She didn't look as guilty as he would like. She just looked bored, resigned to a car ride, and more than ready to go home.

He wasn't sure what she had done today or why, but he wasn't ready to talk about it either, so he turned on the car and pulled away from the newly cleansed property.

Chapter Four

Benedict reached their apartment in the city, the chill of the creek still clinging to his skin. In fact, he felt as though it was a haunting all its own—icy fingers of a dead winter having sunk down into flesh to wrap around his bones. He left a puddle where he stood in the elevator and ignored the glare of his nosy neighbor two doors down.

It wasn't exactly that he was cold, not really, but the memory would not fade, and by the time he got into his apartment, he decided his only choice was to melt the ice in his head. He abandoned his clothes in a wet pile in the bathroom, and then he stood under the spray until the whole room was choking on steam. He wanted to feel uncomfortably warm, right down to his bones. And it worked. Soon enough, he was sweating and thirsty, his brown skin flushed with heat. But even when Benedict drove out the memory of the cold, he could not forget the helpless terror of drowning so close to the surface—or the look on Emmeline's face, just watching him die.

He pushed back his wet hair, away from his face, squeezing his hands against his scalp to press the water from his dark strands. Still standing in his shower, the glass wall thickly fogged, Benedict finally asked, "What happened?"

She didn't answer.

He pushed open the door, steam gushing out. Emmeline sat there on the marble counter of the bathroom sink. She tipped her head from one side to the other and kicked her naked heels thoughtfully.

One morning, just after his eighteenth birthday, Benedict had found her in his room. The first thing he'd heard was her sobs, muffled even though he saw her curled up in the corner. For the first few weeks, she wouldn't talk to him, and when she finally did scream and cry at him, her words were mangled into nonsense. He had left his family home, a part of him hoping to leave her behind as well, but she had followed him to university. She hadn't seemed any happier about it than he was. Eventually, she'd stopped crying, but she still hadn't liked him. She spent that whole first year glaring at him, moving his keys, breaking his phone, ripping pages from his books, and snoozing his alarms.

They had come a long way since then. They were friends now. Partners in life and death.

"Em?" Benedict asked, voice a little harder this time.

She glanced up through her lashes, and then her mouth smoothed into a little smile, mischief gleaming in her eyes.

She ran her gaze down his naked body. She was going to flirt or say something lewd to try to make him smile. It might even work. He had never liked being at odds with her, always quick to make amends.

"We should talk about this," he pressed before she could joke, stepping out of the shower and closer to where she perched. He grabbed a towel from the rack and started drying off. They couldn't escape each other, and after all these years, Benedict didn't want to get rid of her. He couldn't imagine a life without her. "Did you tell that ghost to kill me?"

She straightened suddenly, all amusement draining from her round face. *"I..."* she started but stopped, skin losing color, turning a sickly, dark shade of gray. A large bruise grew across her right cheek, spilling out of a suddenly swollen and purple eye socket.

Benedict walked up to her, standing in front of her knees. He would pass through her if he leaned any closer, but neither of them liked the reminder that they couldn't touch.

"I don't know," she confessed in the smallest voice.

He wanted to argue, to demand a better answer, but it wouldn't have been fair. As much as he liked to think about Emmeline as his best friend, his roommate, and his partner, she was also dead.

Benedict had grown up in a family of spiritualists, known for generations to commune with ghosts and usher dangerous spirits on to the afterlife. Ghosts couldn't always communicate. Many couldn't even interact with the living world, let alone understand it in terms of present day versus past, completely unaware of the difference between living and dead. Emmeline was something special—he knew it, and so did she.

Even when she began to reply to him, to soften a little… Even when they were friends, she still did mischievous things on occasion.

After university, Benedict found an apartment in the city. Emmeline had already helped him fool his brother into believing he had the family gift a few times, so when he was sent to investigate a haunting, it had come naturally that she would relay the information to him. Emmeline told him about any spirits in the room and what messages they wanted to convey to the living. It kept them in the good graces of his family and allowed them access to the Lyon accounts for their bills.

"Okay," Benedict uttered the word to bring peace back between them. He wouldn't say he forgave her because he knew she would take offense. She had not apologized for anything, and he absolutely *knew* she wasn't sorry. He looked down at her hands in her lap. When her mood darkened, the bruises and scrapes came out, her shins covered in dark splotches and her knees bloodied. Some of her fingers were broken, her wrists ringed in rope burns, and her palms torn open from a struggle. One side of her face swelled, bruising and splitting open where the flesh bulged under her eye.

And then, just as the first red buds of blood began to appear on her dress, nowhere near their full size, everything unpleasant began to fade—receding from view and returning her to vivid colors, that clean cotton dress, and unmarred, though eternally ashen brown skin.

Emmeline couldn't lie. No ghost could. And aside from that, her appearance gave it all away.

He touched the counter on either side of her hips and leaned in, close but never touching, leaving the illusion that maybe this time they could. "What should we name him?"

She smiled slowly, and it warmed his heart more than the hottest shower ever could. *"The Winter Spirit?"*

He wrinkled his nose, pushing off the counter and marching out of the bathroom. "That's too dignified for this one! The Axeman? Like Snowman..."

"I think that one's taken," Emmeline said, following him to his room.

He left the doors open because she liked pretending she wasn't a ghost at home. "No, it isn't. We've never named a ghost The Axeman..." Benedict said, less sure with each word.

"No, we haven't, but there was a serial killer by that name."

"Oh." He laughed, having completely forgotten. "All right. How about Mister Ice?" He smiled to himself, tossing his towel into the hamper and dressing in a clean pair of jeans and a t-shirt—not quite as formal as he'd wear out of the house.

"Ugh!" she made a gagging sound. *"That's so unimaginative! The last one was The Butcher's Damsel! How can we go from that to Mister Ice?"*

"Frosty?"

She squished her face into a comical scowl.

"Okay. *Okay.* The Winter Spirit, it is," he conceded, going to his desk and sliding out the drawer. A leather-bound notebook rested inside, a handful of pens rolling around in the space around it. He pulled it out, flipping it open. It had been her idea to keep note of all the ghosts they sent away from the living world. She had come up with it on a whim, he suspected, maybe out of boredom or maybe to see if he would really do it. They had been naming the ghosts ever since, jotting them down together. He did the writing, of course, but she helped with the wording.

The doorbell buzzed before he could sit down.

They exchanged curious glances. Emmeline shrugged with disinterest, and Benedict left the room. He didn't invite people over to his apartment. The only ones that ever rang the bell were fast-food delivery and the occasional nosy neighbor. He had a habit of being a bit of a hermit, and the widow two doors down liked to check on him. Really, he suspected she was just checking on his apartment. She always tried to come inside and look around.

He was sure she would be disappointed if he ever let her past the door—which he didn't. His apartment was modern and sparse. The only room with any clutter to speak of was Emmeline's, and he certainly wasn't going to let anyone else in there. He tugged her door shut on his way down the hall, hiding what was very obviously a woman's bedroom. She had picked out all of her furniture and possessions. She was entitled to a portion of their earnings since she did a great deal of their work, after all. He wasn't always sure it was good for her, though, having that room. It had been fun in the beginning, when he set up the four-post bed and laid out the bobbles and makeup on the vanity just like she'd asked. But sometimes he found her just standing in there, looking like death and staring transfixed at her closet with all the things she had selected for herself but could never actually use.

Emmeline had at least a dozen pairs of the same black ankle boots in there, boxes on top of boxes, with one or two shoes set out. Her ghost was barefoot; he supposed that meant she had died that way. He had asked once why she always picked the same style, and Emmeline had given a little shrug and sigh, *"Because I want them."* And there had been so much honest want in her voice that he didn't press anymore. She wanted her shoes, and he didn't have the heart to point out that she couldn't wear them no matter how many she bought.

Benedict swung out of the narrow hall and turned toward the front door, the living room and kitchen still dark. He opened the door, not sure who he expected, but surprised all the same.

His eldest brother, Elysium, stood in the hallway. His

hands were in his pockets, matching jacket unbuttoned and black vest perfectly snug. Benedict did not like how similar their work attire was. He hadn't realized he was imitating his brother until just now—probably because he hadn't actually seen him in four years, not since the last time Elysium swung by to check up on him. But, of course, for Elysium, it wasn't work attire—he dressed this formally all the time.

Elysium was nearing forty, fit, and teetering between handsome and beautiful. He had a casual authority about him, putting anxious people at ease and gently commanding every room he walked into. He was the golden child of the Lyon family, the heir to the spiritual throne—if there were such a thing.

"I thought you'd still be at the Whittle house," Elysium said, deep voice offering no suggestion of opinion one way or the other.

Benedict remembered his manners, plastered on a smile, and took two steps back from the door. "I didn't know you were on your way or I would have waited. The job wasn't so big that I couldn't handle it." He gestured for his brother to enter.

Elysium walked in, casually surveying the apartment, as though not to judge it though they both knew he couldn't help himself. "I never doubted you, Benny. I am just surprised how quickly you managed it. And from what Henry said—"

"Henry?"

"Mister Whittle." Elysium ran his dark gaze over Benedict. He had lost points in this inquiry for not knowing the man's first name, it seemed. "It sounded like quite the ghost. I heard you were thrown from a window."

Benedict laughed before he could stop himself. "Did you come to check on me? You know I had to have seven stitches after that haunted farm upstate, right?"

Elysium appeared unimpressed. "How do you do it?" he persisted instead. "Everyone else has to have some sort of tact, some charm or clever ploy to get a ghost to give up their name. But not you. You're something of a sledgehammer, baby brother."

Benedict noticed that Elysium hadn't turned on any lights or looked for a place to sit, loitering in the foyer instead. "Oh, I don't know if that's so special. You and Mother have never been particularly charming or cunning about it. You usually just wear the poor bastards down. Perhaps bluntness is a family trait."

Elysium stared back at him, surprised for a moment, and then said, "You need to come home for a few days."

Benedict blinked. "See, there's that family bluntness. Why on earth would I go back to the house?"

"Mother is dead."

Benedict wished they had gone into the living room and sat down. His mother, Gloria Lyon, had never been a warm person, not as he had known her anyway. She had another life outside of the family, he was sure; they all did. But the woman he had known had been all business, all about preparing her children to be honorable examples of the family name and history.

"How?" he managed the only question.

"Lung cancer. It developed quickly. She decided against treatment."

Benedict wanted to be angry. No one had told him, but that was about right. He wasn't sure he would have phoned any of his relations if he had been the one dying.

"The family is gathering for the funeral to make sure her soul is at rest," Elysium went on, making it sound as though it would be a particularly large gathering when, in fact, the family had dwindled down to eight members— now seven. At twenty-eight, Benedict was the youngest of his siblings and cousins.

"Okay," Benedict said feebly, not sure what else to ask. He hadn't been a part of a family funeral, not really. The last one had been his Aunt Vendean, and he had been four years old. He vaguely remembered a séance in the parlor, but that could have been any other occasion. His family had a habit of performing séances. It was there version of watching sports.

Elysium lingered a second longer, as though searching for something else to say. Finally, he turned toward the door. "I will be returning to the estate at once, but I booked you on a flight this evening so that you can pack. I'll send you the info."

Benedict rolled his eyes freely while his brother had his back turned. Elysium was the king of micromanaging.

He would never leave it up to Benedict to get himself home. At least they weren't flying together. "I suppose you'll send a driver to pick me up, as well?" he asked, his tone an expert imitation of the other man's—minus that elusive authority, of course.

Elysium paused in the doorway, glancing back at him with the smallest of smiles. "A car will be waiting, but I assumed you'd rather drive yourself. Why inconvenience a driver with the trip back from the estate?"

Benedict prickled, irritated that his brother managed to know him so well. They weren't close, more than a decade between them and very little other than their disturbing childhood in common. But Elysium had many tricks, not least of them was the ability to take measure of the people around him.

"I will see you at home, baby brother," the eldest said before turning down the corridor. He took the stairs instead of the elevator.

Benedict waited in the doorway until he couldn't hear the other man's shoes in the stairwell.

His mother was dead.

Lung cancer.

It was almost laughable, wasn't it? That a woman who had combated spirits her whole life, survived houses that had claimed lives, and put the most volatile to rest—would die of something so painfully human?

"Are you okay?" Emmeline asked when he closed the door. She chewed her lip, lingering in the mouth of the

hallway.

Benedict nodded stiffly. "We weren't close." She would know that. He had barely spoken to his mother since he left home. He had not been back, and she had not paid him any visits at school or in the city where he settled.

"Still..."

He sighed and sulked past her into the hallway. He pushed open her bedroom door on the way but walked to his own room, falling face-first onto his bed. "We weren't close," he said again, this time wondering why those words were supposed to make him feel better. They just made him feel worse. She was dead, and he didn't even know how to react.

Emmeline crawled onto the bed. It didn't sink under her weight. The covers didn't move. She lay down beside him, looking back at him. If she could breathe—really breathe—he would feel it against his lips. *"I'm sorry,"* she whispered.

They were quiet for a long time. He thought about going to sleep, but his phone vibrated on the table, no doubt with his flight information. He didn't get up to check it. Not just yet. "What was your mother like, Em?" he asked. He never had before. They never talked about her life.

"My mom?" The words broke a little in her throat, like she had forgotten she had one. Maybe she had forgotten. Ghosts were strange things, remains of a person stuck in the world for some cruel reason. *"She was nice. Is nice, I guess. She's probably still alive."* Her voice got smaller and smaller,

eyes glassy. *"She worked all the time, and life was hard for her, but we didn't see it when we were kids. She made sure we didn't see it. I think I only saw her cry twice. One time was when her friend moved away. The other family came by our house to say goodbye before leaving town, all piled into their big car and a moving truck. My mom stood there in the street and stared after the vehicles, tears in her eyes. I didn't understand then what it must have felt like, to have a close friend—a person that really knew her and could sympathize with her—leave. Friendship was a given when you were a kid. They came and went and came again, and it wasn't so hard because there just wasn't much to us yet. We didn't need someone to understand us yet because we were narcissists that believed everyone was just like us."*

Benedict huffed a laugh. He put his hand on the bed between them. She put her hand beside his, their pinkies almost overlapping. "And the second time?"

"Hmm? Oh. My parents had this blowout argument, and my dad stormed off. He did that. He left, but he always came back eventually. I went into my mom's room and found her lying on the bed, crying. I couldn't have been more than ten years old. I didn't know what to do. She was always the strong one. Everyone else was an emotional mess, but not her. She knew what to do. But there she was, broken-hearted. I asked if she wanted something to eat. I think I wanted to offer her something, to make contact, to comfort somehow, but I was too young to know how. I mean, even my food-making abilities were limited to the microwave or stove-top mac and cheese." She darkened, staring at where their hands lay on the covers. He followed her gaze in time to see the bruises forming.

"Do you think she knows I'm dead? Like, feels it? I wonder how much she's cried now…"

Benedict's eyes stung. "I could look her up for you. We could look you up and see if they found out who… That you were…"

"Murdered," she said it. She had never said it before. His gaze flicked back up to her face, expecting to see that ghoulish corpse of a girl beside him. The bloodstains and bruises were gone. Her round cheeks rose in a little offering of a smile, appreciative as though he had done something acutely kind. *"No one knows. No one found me."* She said the grim truths as though they were soothing.

"How do you know?"

Threads of that toxic, violent green swirled in the deep grays of her eyes. *"I know. No one will ever find me."*

His heart broke a little. "I found you." It wasn't the same. He knew that. He hadn't found her body…hadn't solved her murder or stopped it from happening. He didn't even know her full name. But he had found a piece of her, and that piece could never be lost again.

They were quiet for a while longer before she said, *"We shouldn't go—to the funeral, I mean. They might figure your little scam out."*

Benedict huffed. "Elysium has never managed to sense you, let alone see you. I think we'll be fine."

She raised a brow. *"It's a house of ghost hunters. What if they do see me?"*

"They won't."

"What if they do?"

"Then we'll leave." When she didn't reply, he closed his eyes. His mother was dead. The world had changed, and yet, it hadn't. Not really.

"I have a bad feeling," Emmeline whispered.

Benedict smiled softly, sadly, because so did he.

"If we go into that house, we'll never get out again."

He cracked his lids and found her staring back at him. Her eyes weren't the bright green he had expected. She wasn't angry. She was…worried? "I won't let anyone exorcise you. I swear. I won't leave without you."

Somehow, she grew sadder, tears gleaming in her eyes and very nearly overflowing her lashes. And yet she smiled, the way that betrayed the age of her appearance and screamed just how deeply she loved him. *"I know you won't leave without me. You can't."*

Chapter Five

Benedict took a cab to the airport. He only packed one bag, small enough to carry onto the plane, but put it in the trunk rather than the seat beside him. Emmeline sat on that seat—even if the driver didn't see her there.

She leaned forward; another inch and her face would go through the glass partition and into the front seat. She enjoyed snooping because no one but Benedict could see her doing it. She would read every text message and judge every receipt she spotted. She even broke her personal rule of not passing through walls and closed doors when her curiosity got the better of her. There wasn't a neighbor on their floor whose apartment she hadn't nosed around.

"He has an awful lot of receipts for strawberry smoothies…" Emmeline said, true to form.

Benedict smiled to himself, turning his head to glance out the window at the traffic. He wore earbuds when he was outside the house for anything but work; it made talking to her and laughing at her easier.

She sat back and sighed loudly. *"Blow off the funeral. Just get on any other flight."*

"Can't," he said.

The cabby glanced back at him in the rearview mirror, an eyebrow raised.

Benedict tapped one earbud, and the guy nodded, attention back on the street ahead.

Emmeline turned sideways to stare at him. *"What did she ever do for you?"*

He laughed, smile staying even when the sound faded. "Well, she did give birth to me…and then fed and clothed me. Paid for my very useless education and then threw large sums of money at me to keep me in the family business."

"Exactly! She did it all for her own reasons."

"It's not really about her, Em. It's a tradition. It's for the family."

She clicked her teeth and crossed her arms. *"You're going to regret this,"* she mumbled, and he wasn't sure if it was a warning or a threat.

He couldn't stare at her long without the driver's gaze narrowing at him in the rearview mirror.

Soon they were pulling up along the drop-off platform at the airport. Benedict paid with his credit card on the little screen built into the back of the seat in front of him. He tipped generously and got out, holding the door open a few seconds after stepping onto the sidewalk to give Emmeline the chance to slide out after him. He got his bag from the trunk and started toward the crowded doors and snaking lines feeding passengers to automated check-ins and baggage drop-off.

"Bet you're flying first class…" Emmeline said in a bitter mumble.

Benedict nodded once. "Always."

She snorted, keeping step at his side and weaving around people rather than passing through them.

He had never figured out if she sulked over his first-class tickets because she thought it was excessive, or because she couldn't come with him. She never made it past the boarding ramp, vanishing somewhere along the way. The first time it had happened, he had been glad to be rid of her, but then she had popped up again in baggage claim.

Now, Benedict hated flying. It was lonely without her. He didn't know where she went or why she couldn't stay with him—and Emmeline had never explained beyond confirming that ghosts don't fly on planes.

Benedict slid past the lines and right up to the first-class counter. He handed his ID to the man in the blue jacket on the other side of the desk. It took all of two minutes before he had his boarding pass, declining to check his bag.

He turned and paused, gaze combing through the crowd to find her. Emmeline hadn't strayed far, crouching in front of a stroller to look at the baby inside. It blinked up at her with big, brown eyes, spit bubbles slowly growing on its lips and then popping. It saw her. Babies, along with some animals, did.

Benedict hesitated, unable to walk over and talk to her without alarming the parents currently focused on maneuvering their suitcases, toddler on a leash, and stroller in the snaking line toward the baggage drop.

He had to walk away and trust that she would follow. A decade with her had taught him that she would—she always did—whether or not she wanted to. But a flutter of panic still rose in his throat when he turned away from her and slipped into the first-class security line. It was short and fast, and when he emerged on the other side, picking up his bag from the conveyor belt of belongings, Emmeline was waiting there.

Benedict put his earbuds back in, pocketing his phone and wallet.

She stared straight at him, and he stared back.

"Did you ever travel?" he asked.

"Only once," she said. *"They put me in a car and drove me to my death."*

He took steps closer to her, the world moving around them in a rush to catch flights or grab that coffee fix before lift-off. "We could go somewhere—anywhere you want, after the funeral."

Emmeline's lips twitched, but he couldn't tell if it would have been a frown or a grin if she hadn't reined in the gesture. *"You're going to miss your flight,"* she said, voice flat and a storm of electric green gathering in the depths of her dead eyes. She was daring him to go through with it... daring him to get on that plane and drag them both back to his family home.

He stared at her long enough to see the shadow of bruises skitter across her skin, there one second and gone the next.

Benedict nodded once. So, this was how it was going to be? She was going to be angry at him for doing what he had to? He set his jaw and turned, walking away from her and into the labyrinth of high-end shops, cafes, and gates. She would forgive him when this was over and they were home again.

Chapter Six

Benedict drove down the long dirt road between thick woods. The sun gleamed through the branches, casting shadows on the cornflower blue hood and across the windows.

Emmeline sulked in the backseat beside his duffle bag. She hadn't said more than a word at a time in answer to him during the ride to the estate. It was almost three hours from the city. He had left the highway an hour ago and taken to the dirt road. Strange, that he could be gone for so long but still know the way without checking for directions.

He glanced at her in the rearview mirror. She didn't look angry, but she was far from her usual self. She studied the trees outside with a strange mix of wonder, terror, and familiarity.

"Em?" he asked.

She hummed softly in reply, still watching the woods. There were deer out there, hidden in the thick of the trees.

His sister, Lucy, had frightened him as a boy with stories of wolves—stories that harkened to fairy tales. She had been so gifted in her terrorizing that Benedict had refused to wear red until he was fifteen and, even then, never in the woods.

"How did you end up in my house?"

Her head turned suddenly, and for the first time all day, she met his gaze. *"What?"*

"The first time I saw you, you were in my room, crying. But our nearest neighbor is more than an hour's drive, and the highway is almost as far…" He wasn't sure how far he intended to go with this inquiry. Had she been killed in the woods somewhere between the highway and his family home? Had she run from her attacker? Had she wandered as a ghost until she found him?

"Oh," she said, sitting stiffly. *"I don't remember going to your room. I think I was drawn to you."*

He nodded slowly, but he didn't really understand. He had never understood.

"Will all your family be there?" she asked. Was she changing the topic?

"Yeah. We aren't that many, though. No one brings their significant others home. If they have any, they leave them someplace else—someplace away from the estate. No one is family unless they have the Lyon blood." He recalled a heated argument between Lucy and his mother once when she wanted to bring her girlfriend to the house. "So, it was just my mom, her brother, Vernon, and his two kids, and then Elysium, Lucy, Luis, and me."

They drove out of the woods and into a clearing, the Lyon family home far from the reach of branches. He had thought of it as a castle when he was a boy. Three stories of brick with big windows, balconies, and glass doors opening onto stone-laid trails between rose bushes and gnarled, little apple trees.

The front doors opened, and two staff members stepped out, waiting for his arrival. Elysium joined them on the landing at the top of the steps.

"Everything is going to be okay, Em," Benedict promised one more time. "If anyone sees you, or even feels you, we'll leave."

She didn't reply, and he pulled up in front of the house.

The two footmen hurried down the steps, one ready to park the car while the other sought to take his bag. Benedict stopped him before he reached for the trunk and shook his head. "I travel light. It's just the one," he said, pulling his duffle from the backseat. Emmeline looked up at him, a stolen glance now that she was to be unseen. He stepped back, holding the car door open and masking the moment it took her to step out as a chance to stretch his back. Emmeline didn't need him to hold the door—she could pass through walls if she wanted—but it was a habit he would not willingly abandon. It had become his way of acknowledging her even when he interacted with a world that didn't see her. He saw her.

"You made good time," Elysium called from the top

of the stairs.

Benedict didn't fight when the footman took the bag from his hand. They both knew he could carry it himself, but Elysium ran a tight ship, and there was no reason for Benedict to rock the boat.

He took the stairs two at a time. "Am I the first to arrive?"

Elysium's small upturn of lips said it was the opposite. "Uncle Vernon moved into the house a year ago. He lives here year-round now. And Luis was here looking after Mother in her last days," he said, mentioning their other brother.

Benedict nodded. Luis had always been trying to get Mother's love. It was a finite resource in the Lyon house, and everyone knew Elysium would get all she could spare. Everyone but Luis, that is, who thought he had a fighting chance for her favoritism. Benedict didn't need to wonder if he had earned it in those last days. Their mother had probably favored Elysium even more for not staying by her side. She had been a practical woman and would not have liked the waste of time on sentiment.

Elysium led the way into the house, the vaulted ceilings dwarfing the tall doors they walked through. It was all as he remembered it: the checkered marble foyer floor, the wide staircase rising up one side and turning into the second floor of bedrooms, and a pair of French doors to the left leading into the parlor. The windows in that room offered so much light that during a summer's day they did not need electricity. The same couches and chairs stood in the same arrangements. A piano occupied one corner with a round table on the other side of the room for séances and readings. The chirping of birds and the occasional flutter of wings stirred in the three cages hanging, one higher than the other, with their brightly colored finches.

His sister, Lucy, sat at the family séance table playing cards with his cousin, Theodore. Somehow it made sense to see those two being friendly. They had both made spectacles of themselves and the family name. Mother and Uncle Vernon had not approved at first, but they eventually turned a blind eye. Lucy had grabbed up their family history of spiritualism and taken it a small step further, into the occult. She wore black velvet and lace, hanging off her dark shoulders. A thin metal crown ringed her head, pressing down her thick curls. Her long, lacquered, purple nails tapped the backs of her cards. She called herself a witch. Their mother had hated that, but her disapproval had only made Lucy enjoy it more. She read tarot cards for royalty and tycoons now. She rented out castles in Transylvania and held séances. She even had a coven, lining her pockets and devouring her perfect blend of true supernatural and sugary lies.

She twisted sideways in her seat when they walked in. She dropped her cards and shot to her feet. The deck was worn, the black backs rubbed of color by fingers. He caught sight of the ones she had abandoned; the royalty cards were all skeletons in collapsing garb and falling crowns and swords.

"Benny!" Lucy cried, wrapping her arms around him.

Benedict hugged his sister back. He had seen her in December when she had thrown a particularly large, though macabre, gala for her thirty-fifth birthday.

"Well, damn, I lost the bet," Theodore said, cigarette bouncing on his lip while he swept up the cards from the table. He didn't look quite as glossy and perfect as he had on that documentary Benedict caught a few weeks ago, no makeup smoothing out his sharp cheekbones or hiding the dark circles under his eyes. "I didn't expect you to actually show up."

"I didn't know I had an option," Benedict countered.

"You didn't," Lucy confirmed, patting his cheek before going back to the table. She reached out, and Theodore passed her his cigarette.

"I heard you've got a new TV special coming out," Benedict said, crossing the floor to awkwardly shake hands with Theodore. They had never been particularly close. Benedict was evasive, and Theodore wasn't interested in anyone not interested in him.

Benedict made small talk in a room with the three most powerful spiritualists of their time, his relatives, and then glanced up as Emmeline walked around the room. She considered the furniture, the birds in their cages, the old paintings in gaudy frames with the same arched brow and pressed lips as Benedict had worn when examining the Whittle house. He glanced between his brother, his sister, and his cousin, a part of him waiting for one of them to sense Emmeline—to see her, even. But they didn't.

They talked about Theodore's public persona, the soft, understanding medium and how contrary it was to the asshole they had all grown up with. Theodore enjoyed his own duality. "Honestly, I like coming home," he admitted with a wide-lipped grin. "It's the only place I can really be myself. It's exhausting being that good."

Lucy laughed loudly, and Elysium and Benedict smiled.

Emmeline wandered closer, observing them all. *"You smile like him,"* she noted.

Benedict glanced at her before he could stop himself, masking it by pretending to look about the room.

She was still watching Elysium. *"Do you have the same father, or do you both take after your mother?"* she asked, knowing he couldn't answer. Honestly, he wouldn't have known how to even if he could. He had no idea who their fathers were, or who Lucy's was, for that matter. Mother had never said, and he had never heard any of his siblings talk about it. Non-Lyon blood didn't matter. He supposed, though, looking at Elysium, that they did look a lot alike. They were nearly a decade apart in age, but they shared the same build, the same brown skin, dark brown eyes, and delicate jawlines.

"Have you added Mother's picture to the wall, or do we do a ceremony for that?" Benedict asked, trailing from the parlor through the open double-doors and into the large dining room.

"No, Aunt Gloria is up there," Theodore said.

They all followed him, but he only really intended to lead Emmeline. He came to stand in front of the wall of family portraits. The dead were placed here, watching over the living at every meal. It might have felt eerie if the family wasn't all keenly aware when ghosts were actually watching them. That is…all ghosts but Emmeline.

They were better mediums than Benedict by far, and yet, not one batted an eye at the dead girl dancing around them. Were they all faking it like he was? Did they each have a ghost whispering in their ears? Working as their eyes into the spiritual realm? No. If that were the case, Emmeline would see them—and they would see Emmeline.

"I'm surprised she didn't pick a younger photo," Benedict laughed, pointing up at the portrait hung on the wall. Emmeline came close and leaned up on her toes to examine it. The gilded frame had a plaque with the name *"Gloria Andrea Lyon"* and her date of birth and death below. It was a good likeness. Severe. Her silver hair was braided over one shoulder, head turned a little to the side, but her hazel eyes fixed on the viewer with a secret pulling at the corner of her lips. He wasn't sure if she meant to frown or smile. She had been a healthy-looking woman in her late sixties, necklaces weighing down her chest and a stiff jacket holding her shoulders back.

"She was proud to have lived as long as she did," Elysium remarked, standing behind him for a moment to consider the portrait as well. "She said she didn't want anyone looking at this wall in fifty years and thinking at a glance that she had died young."

"Sixty-seven," Lucy remarked, leaning against the dining table. "You know, in most families, that's still pretty young."

"Well, most families don't fight ghosts in their spare time," Elysium reminded.

"And witches," Benedict chimed with a wry smile.

Lucy shot him a glare. "A nasty spiritualist who got herself possessed... Mother never liked when you called that woman a witch."

"But the story sounded better that way," Benedict argued, turning his back on the wall of their relations. "You broke your arm that time, didn't you?"

Elysium smiled tightly, trying not to, maybe. "You were little. I'm surprised you remember."

"I was terrified," Benedict laughed. "Mother dragged me to an old house with a crazy woman and a bunch of ghosts she'd bound to her."

"That's not all she did," Lucy reminded. "She was putting souls into dead things to bring them back to life."

"Trying to," Theodore corrected.

Lucy turned toward him and gawked. "No. She did it."

"No, she didn't," Theodore protested.

"She did," Elysium and Benedict confirmed. Benedict had never recovered from the sight of those undead cats. He still twitched when he heard a meow.

Theodore held on to his skepticism for a second longer before shrugging. "Well, then I'd call her a witch, too."

"Mother said there were no such thing," Elysium maintained.

"She even had a spellbook," Benedict recalled, expecting Lucy to get excited at the reminder and maybe go hunting for the thing. When they had come home from that particularly nasty cleansing, his mother had kept the book and locked it away someplace. Lucy had hounded her for years about wanting to see it.

But his sister didn't light up at the reminder like he had expected. In fact, she stilled, the air pushing from her lungs in one big gush. Everyone froze for a second, and then Theodore blew smoke into thick rings and waved his hand about to dissipate it. "So, if the baby is finally here," he gestured to Benedict, still *the baby* at twenty-eight. "Can we get this funeral rolling?"

"In a rush to get back to Hollywood?" Lucy asked thinly, the punch of her words gone.

"London, actually," he corrected and led the way toward the back of the house.

Benedict turned only partway toward the doors, pausing to look out the big windows at the stretch of land between the house and the woods. He could see the family graveyard from here, made noticeable only by the figures standing in it. The hunched shape of his Uncle Vernon leaned heavily on a cane, staring down at a grave. He assumed it was his mother's freshly covered plot, but really, it could have been anyone. He didn't know his uncle well enough to bet on his sentiments.

"Benedict..." a whisper hissed over his shoulder. He spun toward it, blinking at the empty dining room. Distantly, he heard Lucy, Theodore, and Elysium talking on their way down the back hall. A door opened and closed, and the house fell quiet.

"Benedict." The voice again.

"Em?" He took two steps toward the center of the room. It wasn't like her to play games with him, but Emmeline followed her whims, and he would put nothing past her. He waited, hands balled in his pockets, but the quiet hum of a large house was all that met him. The shuffle of shoes upstairs—probably the staff. A tea kettle in the kitchen, whistling through the walls.

He turned to leave and stopped short, staring at the wall of family portraits. Every single one of them had changed, backs to him, faces hidden. Every one but Gloria Andrea Lyon. His mother's painting stared at him, turned fully forward now. She stared at him, and he stared back, horrified that her image might move or speak. His pulse slammed against his skin, making his temples throb. The paint grew glossy, bubbling at the edges before slowly running. The black of her pupils spread into the dark gray of her irises, staining the whites. Darkness welled in her eyes before finally spilling over, rolling down her face like thick tears of tar.

Benedict shuddered out a breath, unblinking. The paint rolled in globs, gathering against the frame, dragging the color from her cheeks until he saw the white glint of bone beneath.

"Benedict."

He jumped and twisted around.

Elysium stood in the doorway, brow pinching. "Are you okay?"

Benedict looked hurriedly back to the wall, the muscles of his arm jumping, ready to point—but all the paintings were back to the way they had always been. Even Mother's. He coughed and nodded stiffly. Had Emmeline done that? Could she? He glanced out the windows at the graveyard again, swallowing hard when he saw her out there, far from the house, sitting in the grass by the gathering family.

"Are you sure?" Elysium's voice lowered.

Benedict nodded again and hurried out of the dining room and past him, taking long strides through the narrow hall and out the back door.

Chapter Seven

Benedict had never seen anything like that before. Oh, he had heard about visions and the hallucinations ghosts could cause, and he had faked the experience a hundred times, but other than Emmeline, he had never seen anything supernatural except for the occasional levitating object and zombie feline.

His hurried pace only slowed when he neared the graveyard. The grass field stood almost as tall as the old tombstones, kept back from the beds by the groundskeeper. The stones were all similar to one another, though material had changed with the times. No angel statues or heart-shaped marble in the Lyon family graveyard. They knew for a fact that their dead did not reside in this yard, that it was a place for bodies and last rights—to reassure the lingering spirit that all was tended to and that they could move on. After today, the yard would be cared for by the gardeners, kept clean and trim, and no one would visit until the next of them died—probably Uncle Vernon.

He was only sixty-two, but a hard life had left him crooked and tired in a way that left permanent bruises under his eyes.

Luis stood over the fresh gave—Mother's. His eyes were rimmed red from crying, and his light hair was a mess of curls. He was something of the black sheep in the Lyon family, or, in their case, the blond sheep. Aside from being fair skinned and light haired—contrary to everyone else in the family—he was also prone to raw emotions. Today, he looked like the picture of grief, rumpled and drawn.

Strange, that he was the one out of place in this yard. Even Uncle Vernon, her own brother, had no tears to shed. Had dealing with the dead since childhood made them callous to their own? Or did they simply not believe in loss because they knew that souls went someplace else?

Benedict shook the old man's hand, smiling a little when he felt his own grip lacking compared to his uncle's. Uncle Vernon smiled, too, perhaps thinking the same. Benedict's cousin, Hazel, hurried over, cocking her head to the side. She was the model of understanding today, her light-brown hair braided loosely over one shoulder and white, tea-length dress moving in the warm breeze. She was nearing forty and managed to look authoritative and innocent at the same time. Benedict had never figured out how she did it—though she had mastered it since her early teens. Hazel liked to play matriarch whenever Gloria wasn't looking, bossing the rest of them around.

"We're so happy you came home," she said, sounding

very much like the mistress of the estate. He supposed she was the eldest Lyon woman now. Maybe that did put her in charge? He doubted it. Not with Elysium governing over them all in the shadow of their mother. Hazel might lay claim to the estate, with her father to back her up, but she didn't have the natural authority Elysium had. Benedict imagined his brother would even give her reign of the house—like a Pope giving rulership of the land to a King. When the people wanted food, they would turn to her. But when they wanted their souls saved, they knew where to find Elysium.

Rumor had it that Hazel had a couple of kids hidden away someplace. She had never liked the way Mother ran the house—accusing her of being loveless and neglecting her children. With Gloria gone, would Hazel bring her kids to the family home now that no one would interfere in her mothering plans? Theodore, Hazel's brother, had met them on holidays but wouldn't let slip their names, how many, or if they were even her biological kids. When Gloria had pressed for answers a couple of years ago, Hazel had insisted they were the children of her husband and not Lyons. Though Lucy, who spread all the gossip to Benedict's ear, doubted it.

Hazel curled her arm around one of her father's and led him toward the grave. They all gravitated toward it—the fresh mound of soil that weighed their mother down like an anchor in the sea. Lucy, the first to move, laid flowers on the ground and whispered her goodbyes. Theodore put a pack of Gloria's brand of cigarettes down, patting it gently into the soft earth and wishing her well in the next life.

Uncle Vernon shook off his daughter to take the flask from his jacket and pour out a mouthful. "Good job," he said stiffly. Mother had not been the only one with emotional problems in the family.

Hazel dropped a few smooth crystals onto the grave and whispered a prayer.

Luis coughed, choking back tears. Theodore rolled his eyes but turned politely away so that his cousin wouldn't see. Luis crouched down, reaching out to touch the grave. "We miss you so much, Mother," he sniffled, voice raw and so full of emotion that the rest of them took a step back, as though reminded how little they themselves had felt and were burned by it. "You were the strength and the light of this family. You were our compass at sea, always steering us right. I don't know how we'll keep from being lost without you." He stifled a sob.

Theodore caught Benedict's gaze and gestured with a finger gun to his head, blowing out his brains in silent, gruesome pantomime.

"We've always been so close, but I know these last days by your side meant so much to you, and I was so grateful to have them—to drop everything and come home to take care of you."

From the way Lucy and Hazel exchanged glances, they seemed to consider this a direct jab.

Benedict suspected it was more of a boast than an intended insult. Luis had a cloying need to be thought well of—though his efforts often inspired resentment rather than adoration.

"You were the best mother any of us could have asked for, and you loved us in your own way, always making us stronger so that we could hold up the family name proudly and shepherd the lost spirits—"

"*Jesus!*" Theodore finally burst.

Lucy giggled, and Benedict tried his damnedest not to smile.

"You're going to make a ghost out of her if you keep pissing her off like that!"

Luis was still on his hands and knees in the grave dirt, teeth gnashing and body twisting to glare over his shoulder at his cousin. "What are you talking about?"

"You—"

"Enough," Elysium shushed them both and nodded for Luis to finish.

After another five minutes of glorifying their mother, he took out a small pair of scissors and cut a lock of his own hair. He placed it tenderly into the soil and then broke down into dramatic sobs.

Elysium walked over, grabbed Luis by the shoulders, and gently pulled the other man to his feet. He turned him, walking him back a few steps from the grave. They all waited quietly while Elysium patted Luis on the back a few times, head lowered to speak gently but firmly. "Another minute and we'll go inside. Stand," he said.

Elysium straightened his vest when he stepped away. Luis managed to do as he was told, standing on his own.

Benedict caught his eldest brother's gaze. The man nudged his head toward the grave, and Benedict took it as instruction to get on with things.

He dug the coins from his pocket, took one step forward, and tossed them out onto the soil. They sank into the soft ground. He had been thinking about what to say since he got on the plane last night but still didn't have anything. He wouldn't have known what to say if she had been alive—let alone dead. "Goodbye, Mother."

Luis hiccupped behind him.

Elysium patted his shoulder, assuring him it was enough even when it was so little. It was one of the gifts of being the youngest—no one expected much of him.

They all waited, breathless, when Elysium stood at the foot of her grave. He had never been given such a gift as low expectations. He was their mother's protégé since birth— the heir to her imagined throne. For a moment, Benedict was actually impressed. He knew, without a doubt, that he would have crumbled under that sort of pressure, even if he had been a gifted spiritualist like the rest of them. He would have buckled, fought back, rebelled, or just gone mad. But not Elysium. "Sleep well," he said, taking a piece of chalk from his pocket and holding it up as though she were perched on the headstone watching. "Thank you." He tossed it down onto the pile of offerings.

For long minutes, they stood in the silence. He wondered if the others were searching for signs of her by stretching out their otherworldly senses.

Before he could think, he glanced toward the spot where he had last seen Emmeline.

She was still there, at the edge of the graveyard just beside the start of the woods. But she wasn't watching the funeral. She was on her knees, the tiny flower heads on long stalks swaying back and forth beside her shoulders. Her green eyes were focused on the ground, arms stretched out as though she were running her hands along it. He couldn't see clearly from here.

"She would have hated this," Lucy whispered, suddenly beside him.

Benedict looked away from his ghost and met his sister's gaze. Hazel and Uncle Vernon were making a slow walk back toward the house, Luis electing to stay behind and sit with Mother a little longer. Theodore stifled his annoyance with a fresh cigarette pressed between his lips.

"Do you remember when Grandmother died?" Lucy continued.

"No," Benedict answered. Grandmother was but a picture on the wall to him.

"He was still a baby," Elysium reminded.

Lucy huffed a laugh as though he had been lucky not to remember it. "It was terrible. Mother kept rolling her eyes and scoffing until Uncle Vernon finally told her to knock it off. She tossed out the apple she'd been eating in offering."

Benedict jolted at that, blinking at Lucy before bursting into a laugh. "No!"

Elysium cringed but nodded as they started for the house.

"Are we sure Theo isn't one of her kids? Maybe she just didn't want to deal with another one and pawned him off on Uncle Vernon?" Benedict speculated, casting a glance back toward the spot where Emmeline had been. She was gone.

"Oh, no," Theodore exhaled smoke, catching up to them with a few long strides. "You're not moving me on the family tree."

Lucy gasped in mock offense. "You don't want to be my brother?"

Theodore huffed and stretched one long arm back to point the fingers holding his cigarette at Luis. "I am not going to be brothers with *that*."

Elysium shot him a glare. "Don't pick on him. He's not taking the death well."

Theodore groaned but lowered his arm. "Does he take *anything* well?"

At the door, Benedict looked back at the yard. Luis still stood at the edge of their mother's grave, but he wasn't looking at it anymore. His head had turned, and Benedict could swear that his gaze had settled on that spot near the tree-line where Emmeline had been.

"Can you believe he put a lock of his hair on her grave?

Can you imagine how your mother would have reacted to that show?" Theodore laughed with a shake of his head. "She'd be rolling."

Lucy wrapped her arms around one of Theodore's, leaning against his side. "Even I have to admit it was a bit much… And all that talk about how loving she was? I mean, I didn't *hate* mom, but come one, let's be real—that woman was stone-cold."

Benedict pressed down a smile. "Word choice, Lucy…"

Chapter Eight

After dinner, they lingered at the table, basking in the sense of familiarity without the oppression of their matriarch. No one wanted to say it—how freeing it felt to be in that house without Gloria Lyon. Uncle Vernon had retired early. And Luis had gone upstairs not long after, sullen and mumbling something about heartache and loss.

Theodore pillaged the freezer and returned with cartons of ice cream and a fistful of spoons—the same way they had snuck the dessert as teens at night when the adults were out on a ghost hunt. No bowls meant no evidence.

Elysium told the staff to take the rest of the night to themselves—the Lyons would manage on their own for the evening.

"Okay, so let's hear it," Lucy started, picking up a spoon and dragging the carton of strawberry ice cream toward herself. "Who has kids?"

A stretch of silence spread through the dining room, everyone exchanging glances until at last a few guilty smiles grew on their lips. Hazel, Theodore, and finally, Elysium raised their hands in confession.

Lucy howled laughter. "Theo! You do not!"

Theodore shrugged, opening the chocolate ice cream with brownie chunks. "One. Didn't know about her until she was already six years old. She doesn't live with me, but her mother lets me see her sometimes."

He said it all so casually. Benedict supposed there was no real normal in his family.

Hazel confirmed that her husband's three kids were, as they all suspected, her own. She had just wanted to keep them safe from the Lyon ways.

Elysium was the real surprise, though. Benedict had been sure that if and when Elysium continued the family line, it would be just as Gloria had done—coming home with a baby and no mention of a spouse like it was the most normal thing in the world. They all waited for him to explain, and he let the silence stretch until Theodore was about to burst.

"Two boys. Benjamin and Everest."

Benedict felt Lucy and Hazel glancing his way just when he had been stealing the strawberry ice cream from his sister.

"*Benny?*" Hazel said. "You named your kid after Benny?" she asked Elysium before asking Benedict, "Did you know?"

Benedict shook his head with a shrug and dug into the ice cream. It was the creamy kind, with strawberry chunks, at that perfect point of melting where it had become like soft serve. "Didn't know about anyone's kids."

"We should have a family get together here!" Lucy said. Either sugar hit her hard, or she was honestly excited about this whole nieces-and-nephews business. "We could do Christmas or something."

Hazel nodded. "We should. I was thinking of moving home to look after dad. Jackson's a writer, so he can move anywhere, and the kids would probably love the house."

Theodore laughed, tapping his spoon against the rim of the chocolate ice cream. "Love it? Because we loved it so much?"

She waved off her brother's skepticism, turning toward Lucy. "We'll make it happen. You're seeing someone, aren't you? You could bring them!"

Lucy smiled brightly. "Her name's Alex, and we got married last year."

The table of siblings and cousins let out a cheer of surprise and congratulations. Benedict laughed along with them, eating another spoonful of strawberry and marveling at how little they knew about one another.

"What about you, Benny? Seeing anyone?" Lucy asked, stealing his spoon from him. Though it had been her spoon first, so really, she was just taking it back.

Benedict couldn't stop himself from glancing to the side, at the wall of family portraits and the ghost standing in front of it. Emmeline scrutinized the paintings, leaning close and studying them one at a time. "Yeah," he answered without thinking.

Emmeline turned around, brow raised just as his family cheered in excitement.

"We met in college," he fibbed. "We've been living together for years."

Elysium appeared the most surprised. "I've never seen her."

Benedict shrugged. "It's not like you stay long." He had said it lightly, but his brother still looked the tiniest bit hurt. Why? He had a whole secret family. Was it so unreasonable that the youngest could do the same?

"What's her name?" Lucy urged.

Emmeline came closer to him, head shaking. *"Don't."*

He knew her panic, felt it rising in his own chest. Names had power. Ghost hunters used them to invoke spirits and put them out of the world. "Emily," Benedict lied, easier than even he had expected.

Lucy was ready to dive into more questions when the doors opened and Luis returned to the dining room. They all looked up.

He carried a box in both arms, shoulders still sagging and eyes still teary—the way they had been all day. He was like a human raincloud—reminding the rest of them that they were a bunch of heartless assholes trying to picnic at a funeral.

"I was going through some old things, looking for pictures…" he started.

Theodore shoved a spoonful of brownie chunks and melty chocolate ice cream into his mouth, probably trying to smother any comments bubbling up inside.

Luis didn't notice, putting the old box on the table.

"Did you find any?" Lucy asked kindly. They all knew that photos were rare in the Lyon house. No one had been snapping pictures of their first toddling moments or children's birthday parties or Christmas; Gloria and Vernon had had other priorities. There had been no parties.

Luis shook his head. "No, but I found all this stuff." He brightened a little, pulling the old puzzle boxes and decks of cards from the box.

Theodore stood up, dropping his spoon into the carton and grabbing up one of the decks. "I remember these!"

Benedict groaned. He remembered them, too.

"Odd toys…" Emmeline commented, circling the table to get a look inside the box.

"I hated those!" Benedict said. They had all been to test and build psychic abilities. Cards and lightboxes and impossible puzzles.

Theodore was already flicking the rubber band off the deck and shuffling the large, worn cards. "That's just because you sucked at it."

Hazel pressed her smile back unsuccessfully. "Aunt Gloria would make us sit in the parlor with those cards until we could get five right in a row."

Theodore nodded, shuffling the cards and flashing the images on the underside. Colored pictures, shapes, words, and numbers. "I had the best record."

"Second best," Elysium corrected.

"I had to sit in that parlor for two days straight," Benedict sulked. He had never gotten more than one right at a time, and those rare victories had been sheer luck. Elysium and Lucy would eventually lie and say he'd gotten five. They were all certain Gloria knew, but even she got tired of Benedict crying in her parlor.

"Okay," Theodore put the shuffled deck down.

"No," Benedict whined.

Theodore grinned and picked up the top card. He looked at it once, Elysium and Luis getting a peek at it over his shoulder, and then he stared across the table at Benedict.

"I'm not playing," Benedict persisted.

"Just guess," Lucy urged.

Emmeline walked around to the other side of the table, standing behind Theodore's chair. *"A black heart."*

Benedict sighed, trying to sound annoyed so he wouldn't smile. He had hated this game so much as a kid, and he hadn't even thought about how it would work now. "Heart. Black."

Theodore's eyes went wide, and Luis grinned. He turned the card. Lucy and Hazel cheered on either side of Benedict.

Luis picked up a second card.

Emmeline leaned over his shoulder. *"The number twelve."*

"Really?" Benedict complained when his brother took part in the game. He groaned, nodded, and pretended to think hard. If anything, Benedict had become a good performer during his decade of ghost hunting. "It's a number. Twelve."

Lucy screamed in delight when the card turned. They continued to play until Benedict was up to seven in a row. Should he throw out a wrong answer to end the game?

"What's your record, Elys?" Hazel asked.

"Eleven."

Emmeline grinned. *"We could beat that…"*

Theodore picked up another card, glancing at it quickly and then pressing it to his chest.

"Star," Emmeline said. *"Yellow."*

"A yellow star," Benedict repeated.

Theodore laughed and swore, tossing it down. "When did you get good at this?"

Benedict shrugged. "College. I'm a late bloomer."

"Keep going," Elysium pressed.

They did. He had ten right.

When Theodore reached for the eleventh card, Elysium put two fingers to the top of the deck to stop him. He slid the top card off, face down on the table, and stared across it at Benedict. "Guess it."

Hazel groaned. "That's cheating, Elys. The whole point is to get it from someone else's mind."

Emmeline leaned over the table beside Elysium. And for the first time, it struck Benedict how young she looked. It had been easy to forget that she was unaging, caught forever as a reflection of herself at eighteen, when it had just been the two of them. But seeing here there beside Elysium underlined both the new streaks of gray in his brother's hair and the fact that Emmeline would never catch up. Someday, Benedict would be old and gray, and she would still be the same.

She was so close to Elysium, right beside him, but he didn't notice. How could he not sense her? How had none of them noticed her?

Benedict was about to laugh and toss out a guess when Emmeline reached out. Her fingers touched the top of the card, almost touching Elysium's digits. She stared hard at it and then grinned, looking up at Benedict. *"It's a rose. And that one,"* she pointed at the top of the deck. *"Is a raindrop."*

Benedict wanted to ask her how she knew, but Emmeline's vision was different than his—than any of theirs. As much as she appeared to be here with him on this plane, she was someplace in between, overlapping places and times. He stood and stretched like he might leave without guessing. His family held their breaths, about to complain.

"It's a rose."

Lucy made her excited, humming sound, heels beating a drumroll on the floor until Elysium flipped the card.

Theodore shouted, smacking the table.

Benedict grinned and walked down the side of the table to reach the deck. He didn't break eye contact with Elysium. "Raindrop," he said and flipped the next card.

Even Luis let out a peal of laughter, the room erupting with squeals of delight as he called the twelfth card in a row.

Elysium's hard expression pulled suddenly into a grin. "Well, damn." He laughed and fell back into his seat. "Maybe the rest of us should still be practicing…"

"That's some serious ugly-duckling-turning-into-a-swan shit," Theodore said.

"We shouldn't have second-guessed him," Hazel chuckled. "He's been hunting ghosts for years. It's just hard not to think of him as our little runt anymore." She managed to make it all sound sweet, and Benedict laughed.

But he noticed Emmeline wasn't laughing. She was back to lurking in the corners, stalking the room and watching all of them with her mysterious green gaze. He was so used to her that he easily forgot how strange this was. And the only ones he could ask about Emmeline, about how she could exist without anyone but him seeing her, and why he could see only her and no other ghost, were the very same people he could never tell. His family believed he was normal now, normal like them, and they had made a life out of pushing spirits from their world on to the next. No, he could never tell them. He supposed that meant he could never know why she was here—a small price to pay to keep her.

Chapter Nine

Benedict woke suddenly that night. He sat upright in bed, staring at the darkness of his room and waiting—listening. Something had pulled him so completely from sleep, and yet he couldn't remember what it was, his heart beating wildly in his chest.

A heavy *thud* came from downstairs, making him jump where he sat.

He pushed back the covers and turned on the bedside lamp. 12:14 a.m.

Another *thump*. A door slapping against a wall?

Emmeline stood beside the doorway, staring at him. She hadn't made an appearance since the game with the cards hours ago. *"Don't go,"* she whispered.

Another *thud.* Someone hitting the wall? Or stomping on the floor downstairs?

Benedict pulled on a t-shirt and padded barefoot toward the door. "What is it?"

"Don't go," she repeated, eyes big and head shaking.

"Don't look."

A chill ran up his spine, and he hesitated at the door, staring at the knob. They had been through at least a hundred hauntings and séances together. What could be worse in his own house? What would he see that could be that bad?

Another *thump* downstairs. He threw the door open and hurried into the dark hall. Elysium and Lucy emerged from their rooms almost at the same time.

"Go back to bed," Elysium said to them both, first to the foyer.

Neither listened.

The *thudding* grew louder on their path to the dining room.

The scent of cigarette smoke made Benedict's stomach knot. It wasn't the brand Theodore smoked—it was their mother's favorites. Elysium paused at the doors, and Benedict knew it must have hit him, too. And then he threw them open and they were all marching into the lit dining room.

Lucy inhaled so sharply that her whole body jerked back a step.

A woman sat on the dining table, arms gloved in fresh blood up to her elbows. Thick sprays of red speckled her face and neck, staining the front of her uniform. She stabbed a long kitchen knife into the table beside her thigh, fingers twisting around the handle. She stared, unblinking, at the wall of family portraits in front of her.

A thick smear of blood colored the floor where a man had fallen and dragged himself to the other side of the room.

Shaking, he reached up, smacking his palm to the wall once more in a desperate plea for help.

"Lucy," Elysium called their sister but didn't take his eyes off the woman. Lucy hurried across the room. She grabbed the man by the shoulders and turned him over, soft assurances flowing from her lips like a sweet river.

It was the same man who had carried Benedict's bag into the house yesterday. His shirt and vest were soaked with blood, more bubbling up from his lips when he tried to speak. Lucy pushed her hands against his stomach to stop the bleeding, but it came up faster for her efforts, leaking between her fingers.

"What have you done?" screamed the woman sitting on the edge of the dining table.

Benedict and Elysium jumped at the sudden outburst, but she wasn't looking at them.

Her mouth opened wide, dragging in a breath that shook her where she sat. *"What have I done?"*

She stared at the family portraits, tears streaming down her face, dragging the spray of blood into thin streaks of pink.

"Madam?" Elysium spoke, voice stern, one hand out in a calming gesture.

She began to turn toward him, but her attention snagged on Benedict. He held his breath when he met her gaze. There was something alarmingly familiar about the way she stared at him. Her expression softened, tears still bright in her eyes and her mouth trembling. *"I did it for you, boy,"* she whispered.

Elysium made a choking sound—it was the first time Benedict had ever heard it. He grabbed Benedict's arm and pulled him a step back and behind him. "Mother?" Elysium said loudly.

Her gaze slashed to him, lips curling. She pulled the knife from the table and slid from the edge, landing on her feet in the puddle of blood. It dripped from her, oozing out of the gashes in her uniform.

"Holy shit," Benedict hissed. "I think she stabbed herself…"

The woman ignored him. *"She's still here,"* she told Elysium, voice distorting, and Benedict could almost hear it—almost hear their mother's voice echoed in this woman's throat. *"What did we do?"*

"Mother, please," Elysium tried to soothe. "Look at what you're doing. These people don't deserve what's happening."

She blinked back at him almost lazily, head tipping to one side. *"No one's getting out. Not them. Not you. Not him."* She cut her gaze to Benedict, and he jumped.

"Enough," Elysium snapped. "You will leave this house. You will not linger and degrade your spirit like this."

"My spirit? Or our name?" she laughed.

Elysium balled his hands, glaring at the woman—through her and into the spirit that infected her. "Get out," he ordered.

Her laugh dwindled, but a smile remained. It was their mother's smile, the sharp one they all knew too well. *"You've met your match, boy. I trained you well. You're better than the rest. But not better than me."*

"Leave this place!" Elysium's voice rose, and Benedict winced back—but the woman possessed by their mother didn't flinch.

"I was wrong, Elysium," their mother said in the cruelest whisper. *"We were all wrong. You're wasting your life, pulling weeds in the forest for gods that do not care. We are bullies, distorting the natural order for our own pride."*

Benedict waited for Elysium to speak, to command her to leave again, but he didn't. His brother stared at the woman, stunned.

"Stop it," Benedict spoke up, trying to step around Elysium, but that jarred his brother, the other man moving quickly to keep him behind. "You're hurting people. You could kill them. Just leave."

She didn't look at Benedict, not even when she spoke. Her gaze was fixed on Elysium, as though she meant to entrance him like a cobra. *"Am I hurting people? Am I killing them?"* she asked, mock sympathy dripping from her words.

A rush of movement across the room drew Benedict's gaze. Lucy was on her knees on the floor, beside the injured man but not tending to him. No, there was no point. He was dead—no longer gasping for air through a mouthful of blood but staring sightlessly at the ceiling, face twisted in terror.

Lucy moved her hands across the seat of a chair, drawing circles and runes with globs of thick, red gore. She wrote something in the middle.

"Wait..." Benedict barely got out the word before she stood, picking up the chair. The light gleamed off the blood she had used for paint, and he saw their mother's name shining there. "It's a possession not—" he tried, but she swung the chair and broke it against the wall.

It wasn't the ghost that screamed—it was the woman she had possessed. Elysium's eyes flared in alarm, and he reached out for the maid, but it was too late. The spirit clung onto flesh and bone, the spell swirling around her in a gale, rattling the paintings on the walls and knocking over chairs. Elysium grabbed her arms, but the wind lifted her, eager to banish the ghost inside. She screamed and screamed until Benedict clapped his hands over his ears. She twisted in the air, and despite all the sounds and his hands pressing over his ears, nothing could mask the snapping of her back. Crack after crack. Her head turned backward, limbs mangled in all directions and flesh split open.

She fell to the floor hard, and her skin and bones smacked the hardwood, echoing through Benedict and down to his gut, dropping him to his knees.

The wind stopped, the room stilled, and the three Lyons stared at the dead bodies.

"Why did you do that?" Benedict whispered, panting for air.

"I had to," Lucy hissed, clawing at the table to drag herself to her feet. Thumping steps upstairs promised that they had awoken the whole house. Everyone would see this soon.

"But you can't drive out a possession like that… You *know* that." How could she not? They all knew. Possessions were not the same as casual hauntings. And a spirit as willful as Gloria Lyon's would not be cast out that easily. They could push her back, but they couldn't banish her with a broken talisman.

"She would have died anyway," Lucy said, voice too weak to enforce any belief behind her words.

"You don't know that!" Benedict snapped, turning on his knees toward his sister. "You accomplished nothing!"

Lucy didn't defend herself like he had expected. She wouldn't even look at him—wouldn't look at either of them or the bodies, her gaze stubbornly piercing the floor at her feet.

"Enough," Elysium said, swallowing hard. He hadn't looked away from the twisted corpse at his feet, hands still out toward it as though reaching for her.

The doors opened, and Theodore rushed in, reeling back almost as soon as he did and colliding with Hazel.

"Get them out of here," Elysium ordered.

Hazel stepped closer, gaze flickering between Lucy, Benedict, and the bodies. "Elys?"

"Them," he clarified sharply, pointing at Lucy.

Hazel nodded once and crossed the room, collecting her cousin by the arm and leading her out of the room.

Benedict felt Theodore's hand on his back before he heard his voice, deep and steady now. He couldn't quite make out the words, though. He couldn't shake the sound of that woman's spine twisting, vertebra grinding and cracking.

"What happened?" Theodore asked, voice hushed as he led Benedict up the stairs.

He didn't remember leaving the dining room, gaze hazy with tears. "She was possessed. We should have coaxed Mother out of her or done an exorcism, not…"

"*Mother?*" Theodore interrupted, steering Benedict down the long hall toward his bedroom. "Aunt Gloria possessed the maid?"

Benedict nodded, remembering the minutes like hours played out frame by frame. "She killed the footman. She was completely mad."

Theodore managed to open the bedroom door without letting go of his iron grip on Benedict's arm, leading him in and pushing him down onto the nearest couch.

Benedict caught his hand before he could step back, looking up at his cousin. "Lucy made a talisman and broke it, driving her out."

Theodore blinked at him. "What? No. She wouldn't do that."

Benedict exhaled, grateful someone else saw how insane the choice had been. "She did."

His face twisted with confusion and worry. "I'm going to go check on her. Stay here, okay?"

Benedict nodded.

"Try to get some sleep. You don't need to come back down. We'll take care of everything."

Benedict almost laughed. The door closed behind Theodore, and he was surprised when it didn't lock. He felt like he had gone mad in a matter of minutes. Somehow being locked up would have made sense.

He dropped his head forward, staring at his hands. They weren't bloody, but a part of him had expected them to be. "What's happening?" he asked, knowing she was with him even before he looked up.

Emmeline shook her head, arms curled around herself. *"We'll never get out. We'll never leave this place."*

Benedict leaned forward onto the edge of his seat. "Was that my mother's ghost? Why would she do that? How could she—"

"We're going to die," Emmeline choked out. *"We're going to die,"* she said again.

What was wrong with her? She was already dead. "Em—"

His door opened, Elysium taking one step in. He paused, glancing around the room and right through Emmeline. "Were you talking to someone? Did Mother contact you?"

Benedict shook his head. "I tried to talk to her, hoping maybe she'd answer..." he lied.

Elysium sighed. "Don't. She's obviously dangerous. Hazel wants to do a séance tomorrow night, to try to draw her out so that we can send her on." It was going to be a long day.

"Why is she here?" Benedict asked.

Elysium's shoulders sagged under too much weight. "I don't know, but we need to get rid of her."

Benedict nodded once. It was then that he noticed his brother slept in silk pajamas, the sort with matching top and bottom. Gray, because he imagined Elysium would think black too formal for sleepwear.

"If you're up for it, you should join us," Elysium suggested.

Benedict nodded again and then jumped to his feet just before his brother could leave. "The staff…the ones that died…"

"I'll call the sheriff in the morning and let her know about the murder-suicide."

He winced at the lacking term. *Murder-suicide.* It sounded like something it wasn't—like the people who had died had any control over the situation—like it wasn't the fault of the Lyons.

"The bodies will be taken to the morgue in town for cremation. Hopefully, the sheriff won't come out to poke around."

"Why wouldn't she?" he snapped, not meaning to sound angry but unable to stop himself. His family had always had a strange relationship with Vannes, the nearest town to their estate. For the most part, the townsfolk seemed to enjoy the mystery and stories of the Lyons, blaming everything from colds and bad weather to missing people on the family of spiritualists. A few times, his mother had called the Vannes Sheriff about town kids coming out to the estate to vandalize the property. But usually, when the sheriff had come out, it had been because of a séance gone wrong, injured guests, and staff fleeing in terror.

Somehow everything would always be smoothed over in the end—no doubt helped by the very competent lawyers the family kept on retainer for just this sort of incident, and the Lyon habit of making large and regular donations to Vannes but never interfering in town business. They never even attended Town Hall meetings.

Elysium sighed, nodding slowly because not even he could believe the sheriff would just ignore two dead bodies without making an appearance. "The rest of the staff are being sent away until we can cleanse the house."

Benedict sank back down onto the couch. Emmeline was beside him now. "Send for me when it's time for the séance," he said, staring straight ahead until his brother closed the door and he could look at his own ghost. "We could leave. Right now," he whispered.

She smiled, the gesture tight with sadness, tears welling in her eyes. They never spilled. He suspected they couldn't. *"It's too late. You're going to die here."*

Benedict groaned and scrubbed his hands over his face. "Can you be less doomsday for a minute?"

She went quiet.

He lifted his head, afraid she had gone. She sat there still, staring at him and not saying anything. And then she cocked an eyebrow, and he realized she was being quiet for a minute to give him one with less doom. He heaved out a laugh that mingled with a sob. Damn, she was dark—he suspected even by ghost standards his Emmeline was grim.

She crossed her arms over her chest. *"You should go,"* she finally said, though she didn't sound convinced he'd make it.

"It's my mother's ghost, isn't it?" he asked quietly, studying her. What he really wanted to ask was if Emmeline had done this. He had seen her in his room while that mayhem began downstairs. She couldn't have been in two places at once—that much he knew.

Bruises moved like shadows over her skin, there and gone. She was a corpse, and then she was a girl again. *"It's her,"* she said quietly.

He sighed and nodded slowly, standing from the loveseat. "We'll stay for the séance then. If you see her... You'll warn me, won't you?"

Emmeline startled, cracking that veneer of spiteful fury. *"Always."*

He nodded and then went to his room and flung himself down on the bed. He laid there on his chest, waiting for her to join him. She did, laying down next to him on her side of the bed. She curled onto her side, staring back at him the way she always did. *Always.* But there was something brewing between them, something gathering in her like a storm that had been there for years. He feared it would be a hurricane when it finally broke free.

"There are things you don't tell me," Benedict whispered sleepily, so tired.

"There are things you don't understand," she countered. She wasn't tired, but she wasn't entirely present either.

He closed his eyes. "Will I understand when I'm a ghost, too?"

She didn't answer. Or maybe he fell asleep before she did.

Chapter Ten

Benedict woke around nine in the morning, showered and dressed, and snuck out of his room. It reminded him of when he was younger, creeping around because he didn't want Mother to spot him and test his lack of abilities.

He paused at the top of the stairs. Hazel and Elysium were arguing in the foyer, voices hushed.

"We need to send him away," Elysium pressed.

"You don't think that'll look suspicious?" Hazel countered.

"It isn't safe for him."

She laughed, and it was an ugly sound. "You mean it isn't safe for you? Just tell him. Who cares if it makes him sad? We did what we had to. We saved his life!"

"Shut up," Elysium snapped when her voice rose. "Something like this could ruin the family."

Benedict wondered if they were talking about Mother's ghost and the dead staff. That seemed pretty scandalous. But who were they worried about finding out? Had they not told Uncle Vernon? Had he somehow missed it?

Benedict was about to go down, interrupt their whisper fight, and ask some questions of his own when Emmeline caught his attention. She stood at the other end of the hall, waving him toward her. When he started walking, she held a finger up to her mouth and pointed at Theodore's bedroom door. She smirked in a very mischievous, up-to-no-good way that both thrilled and worried Benedict. It was the first sign of her acting like her usual self since they got here. She slipped through the closed door, vanishing.

Benedict followed with quick steps.

He didn't knock.

The smell of incense hit him first, the room dark despite the rising sun outside. Heavy curtains had been drawn over the windows and the lamps left off. Dozens of candles were lit and set out along the side tables, casting shadows more than light. Theodore's room had always looked the same—like a guest room. Comfortable and expensive, but far from personal. He had been honing all his personal expression on clothing since childhood—his room had never mattered to him.

"Theo?" Benedict asked.

His cousin sat at the table, slumped over it, forehead to the tablecloth. He didn't move or speak.

"Theo?" Benedict tried again, coming closer. The door snapped shut behind him, but before he could turn toward it, Theo jerked upright—inhaling so deeply that he shuddered in his chair.

His eyes opened, wide and unfocused for a long second.

And then the man laughed, grinning widely. It wasn't his laugh or his grin. He hugged himself, rocking back and forth in the chair.

"What are you doing?" Benedict whispered.

Theodore stood up and stretched. *"He was asking for it,"* Emmeline explained, her voice mingled with Theo's. *"He was begging to talk to a ghost in this house. He even offered himself up as a vessel, looking to understand."* Theodore walked around the table, but his sway and his stride were all Emmeline.

He walked right up to Benedict, standing only inches away, and reached up to brush fingers across his cheek.

Benedict should stop her, and he knew that. It wasn't right. But his pulse jumped at that touch.

Theodore leaned down, plush lips close to his. Heavy lashes lifted to meet Benedict's gaze in the near dark. He saw the swirls of her maddening green in the depths of his cousin's eyes. She kissed him, and Benedict kissed back, sinking fingers into the back of his cousin's hair to hold his face closer, kissing deeper. Emmeline did not taste like he had imagined she would—no sugary coffee or hint of lipstick, but cigarettes and breath mints.

The kiss grew frantic, Theodore pushing Benedict up against the nearest wall and pressing against him. With a groan, Benedict shoved him back and shook his head. "No."

Theodore laughed, but the sound was Emmeline. *"Why not?"*

"You can't use his body like this," Benedict said, breathless. "I can't."

"Because he's your cousin?" she asked, tipping Theodore's head to one side.

"Because he's an unwilling participant. Let him go, Em."

The smile on Theodore's lips withered. *"Why?"* she demanded again, voice darker.

Benedict's head snapped up to glare at the ghost in his cousin's eyes. She had never done anything like this before. She had never possessed anyone. "What's going on with you?"

Theodore took a step back, face still twisted in a bitter scowl.

"Are you doing this, Em? Are you infecting my mother's spirit?"

Theodore took another step back, tears gathering in his eyes.

"You think I haven't seen how you rile other ghosts? I see the way you whisper to them before I get there, before they go violent. If you wanted to hurt me, why not just do it yourself?"

Theodore laughed miserably, tears rolling down his cheeks. *"Oh yes, you see me, Benedict. But just me. Maybe the other ghosts aren't even there. Maybe it's just me. Maybe I'm the only ghost and I've been the one trying to kill you all along,"* Emmeline said.

He was grateful for the wall against his back, holding

him up when his mind raced. He went through all of his memories, searching for the possibility of truth. No. No, she couldn't have been the other ghosts. If he could see her, then she couldn't be someplace else—his mother had taught him at least that much.

She cried angrily, Theodore's fists balled and pushing hard into his own sides. His fingers wrapped around his thumbs—the way she did when she was afraid or sad. *Maybe*—that was how she had said it. *Maybe* she had done it. She couldn't lie, so the closest she could get was leading him to the conclusion himself. "Say it then," Benedict prompted, tears in his own eyes now. "Tell me you're the only ghost. Tell me you've been trying to kill me all these years."

Theodore's lips pressed shut. She couldn't say it because it wasn't true.

"I always thought it was the pain and anger of the ghosts we met that spilled over onto you. I thought it was their temper that affected you when we went out to cleanse properties…"

Theodore stood still, lifting his chin high, and Emmeline peered out from his eyes—daring Benedict to realize the truth.

"It's your anger, isn't it? It's your anger that makes the other ghosts violent."

Theodore sat down, back into the chair where he had started. *"You wanted to talk to ghosts, so I talked to them for you. You wanted to know their secrets, their pasts, and their names—*

and I gave you everything about them. I helped you push them from this world." She put Theodore's hands back on the surface of the table, palms flat. *"You have no right to judge me, Benedict Lyon."* Her gaze cut deep into his soul. *"And I am not sorry for anything."*

Before Benedict could even think of a reply, Theodore's head flung back. His mouth opened wide like he might scream, but he only convulsed before collapsing forward again. His forehead whacked the surface of the table, and the dark room went still again.

Seconds later, his cousin was coughing and sitting upright, rubbing at his head. He started when he saw Benedict there, no memory of him coming into the room—no memory of anything since the moment he went into his trance in search of spirits. "What happened?"

Benedict slid his hands into his pants pockets. "Nothing. I heard you talking to yourself and came in. Jumping the gun on tonight's séance?" He tried to make his voice sound casual.

Theodore swallowed, fingers pushing his hair back into place, away from his face. He had a red mark on his forehead from where it had hit the table. "I guess. What was I saying when you walked in?"

Another shrug. "Couldn't tell. But you probably shouldn't do this again—not after what Mother made that maid do."

Theodore flushed, nodding tightly. "Yeah. Yeah, it was dumb. But Aunt Gloria wouldn't do that to us." He sounded distant, glancing around the room as though almost remembering something.

"I'm going to go downstairs to get something to eat," Benedict said, though he couldn't imagine eating anything right now. "Do you want to come with me?"

Theodore started to nod again before he shook himself out of it, standing from his chair. "Give me a few minutes."

Benedict hesitated, suddenly afraid his cousin really would try his communing with spirits again—and this time, it wouldn't be Emmeline who accepted his invitation.

Chapter Eleven

Benedict stood in the doorway of the dining room, staring in but unable to step through. The bodies were gone, and the floor cleaned. Two deputies were outside, taking photos of a shattered window, the body on the ground near the driveway, and the other laying in the grass.

"You should have called us immediately," Sheriff Martin berated Hazel on the other side of the room. Her deputy, a man in his early twenties who Benedict had never met before, sat at the dining table, taking notes.

Elysium had gone through the story of what happened. And it was a *story* at this point, no longer the truth. Their mother had taught them what parts of the truth to use and what parts to put away when talking to the public. According to Elysium, half the house had woken to the sound of an argument. He and Hazel, not Lucy now that she was hiding away in her bedroom, had rushed downstairs and out the front door to find the maid, Amelia Jane, with a kitchen knife. Elysium said the woman had been in tears, screaming and flailing the knife about, and that she had attacked the footman, John Moreau. When he and Hazel tried to help Mr. Moreau, Miss Jane ran away, back into the house and upstairs.

Hazel took over the story at that point, claiming to have run up the stairs after the maid, horrified to find her in the study, stabbing herself with the kitchen knife. When Hazel tried to stop her, she jumped out the window.

Benedict listened to them repeat the story four times, never missing a step—never forgetting a detail no matter how the sheriff turned her questions. He wondered how long it had taken them to move the bodies, to come up with their story, and clean the rest of the house. Which one of them had created a blood trail up the stairs? Which one had thrown Amelia Jane's already broken body out the window?

And whose idea had it been to talk in the dining room, where the murders had actually occurred? Was it a coincidence? Had the sheriff chosen the spot? Or had Hazel and Elysium been that cocky?

"We were in shock," Hazel said, batting eyelashes that only barely held back her tears.

Sheriff Martin glared at her, rolling her jaw from side to side thoughtfully. She wasn't buying Hazel's act. Sheriff Martin had been a deputy when Benedict left home, and he wasn't the least bit surprised to see her in charge now.

"My mother passed away recently. We just came home for the funeral," Elysium explained. "This was a lot to take in, and we didn't want my uncle to wake up to police in his home and dead bodies outside. His health hasn't been well. We thought maybe we could wait a few hours to gentle the blow. We did put sheets over the bodies and closed off the upstairs study."

Sheriff Martin appeared monumentally unimpressed. "I've met Vernon Lyon," she said, deadpan. "I doubt all the sirens in the world would phase him."

Benedict took a step back, stomach knotted, and ready to get as far from this charade as possible.

Just then, the sheriff's gaze snapped to him. "You," she said.

Benedict froze.

Hazel glared at him from behind the sheriff's shoulder, a thousand threats and warnings in her gaze—all sounding something like, "Don't mess this up."

"You were home when it happened?"

"Yeah."

The deputy at the table studied him, and then scribbled more notes.

"You see anything?" the sheriff asked.

"I heard the shouting last night, but when I went to see what was going on, Elysium told me to go back to my room and stay there. So I did."

Sheriff Martin narrowed her eyes on him, staring hard. "You don't look like someone that does what he's told."

Benedict almost laughed at that. "I do when I'm in this house." He swallowed hard when he said it, suddenly worried he shouldn't have. Was he making their home sound dangerous? Wasn't it?

"You have nothing to add?" the sheriff pressed.

"No, ma'am."

She glared but nodded stiffly. It felt like a dismissal, and Benedict was more than happy to go. Another deputy was in the foyer, taking pictures of bloody shoe prints on the glossy hardwood, leading up the stairs.

Emmeline stood to the side, watching the man work with casual disinterest.

"Can I go upstairs?" Benedict asked.

The deputy jumped, clutching his camera in both hands like a shield. He huffed a breath and a thin laugh when he saw Benedict. "Um. Give me another minute."

Benedict nodded, standing back and leaning against the wall. He could go into the parlor. Or maybe just go outside and take a walk and hope all of this disappeared by the time he got back. The others had been smart to stay shut up in their rooms when the police arrived.

"Never thought I'd be inside the Lyon house," the deputy said, taking another picture, the flash flaring through the hallway.

Benedict looked up, surprised.

The deputy continued to work, making his way upstairs one photo at a time. "Sorry. It's just… When I was a kid, we used to dare each other to come over to your house.

We were such chicken-shits; I don't think any of us made it more than two steps past the tree-line onto the property."

Benedict leaned back against the wall. "What did you think would happen if you reached the house?"

The deputy paused midway up the staircase. He glanced at Benedict, and then looked back out the front doors before he could stop himself.

The coroners were putting the first body into a thick plastic bag, struggling to fit her broken limbs inside.

Chapter Twelve

Benedict sat at the table in the parlor with his siblings, cousins, and uncle, marveling at how they had all dressed up. They always dressed up for séances—three-piece suits or gowns. It was their church, he supposed.

They were minutes from midnight, and candles held the room aglow, crowding every surface. The finches chirped to themselves in the cages in the corner. He imagined they found the display unspectacular. They were used to oddities by now. Or maybe they had simply never cared for what happened outside their frail metal bars. Benedict had never seen any sign of interest from them nor any of their predecessors.

He glanced across the table, over Uncle Vernon's shoulder, at the closed doors of the dining room.

Lucy would usually lead the séances. She had a knack for it, or maybe just practiced showmanship in the art, but not tonight. She hadn't said more than a few words since Benedict walked into the room. He still didn't understand why she had created and broken a seal knowing what it would do to that woman. Had she panicked? He had spent a good deal of time today thinking about his sister and her illustrious career as a spiritualist. How much of it was actually dealing with ghosts, and how much was fortune-telling and wowing her audience?

Hazel took his hand, startling Benedict. Everyone followed suit, and soon they were all holding hands at the table and closing their eyes.

Benedict was the last. All eyes had closed but his, and he stole a glance at Emmeline where she sat in the chair under the birdcages. She met his gaze.

"Should I leave?" she asked.

He wasn't sure. Would they sense her if they gathered like this and tried to weed out the ghost in their house? Would they find his ghost instead? Did he dare send her away and go blind into this? He shook his head once and closed his eyes.

Hazel spoke softly, her voice filling the quiet room. "Aunt Gloria," she called. "We know you are in pain. We know you are lost. We will see you safely home, but you must make yourself known."

They waited. Hazel said it again. Another length of silence, and then a third time.

The same words, the same patient tone, and the sense that Hazel would continue to gently demand her aunt's presence until dawn if she was not answered.

"Aunt Glor—"

Uncle Vernon jerked, the legs of his chair sounding on the floor just before he sucked a deep, wheezing breath.

Benedict opened his eyes, staring across the table at the old man sitting between Theodore and Elysium. They had opened their eyes, too.

"I am not alone." Uncle Vernon heaved the words as though they'd come up in coughs from his lungs rather than formed against his vocal cords.

"Is she with you, Dad?" Hazel asked him.

He rattled another breath, eyes unfocused. *"I am not alone. You are not safe. You cannot leave."*

Luis squeezed Benedict's right hand. He had forgotten his brother was there until then.

"Mother?" Luis called, all of his need and heartache cracking his voice.

Uncle Vernon jostled in his seat a little, as though something squirmed inside him. Theodore and Elysium held tighter to his hands, keeping him from breaking the circle.

"Aunt Gloria?" Hazel demanded, voice stern.

Uncle Vernon shuddered, saliva rolling from his mouth and down his chin over his short, gray beard.

"Aunt Gloria, you must leave this place and go on to the next world. You cannot remain. You know that," Hazel persisted.

Uncle Vernon groaned.

No one played at invoking angels or good spirits as they might for an audience. They didn't pit prayers or deities at the ghost. They knew the simple truth of what they did—gifted with sight and strong souls, they threw their will against another until one broke. Together, they had drawn the spirit into the room, willed it to themselves, and now they willed it to speak, to yield, to abandon the living world and vanish. Everything else was showmanship.

"Let go," Emmeline whispered near Benedict's ear, leaning over his shoulder and staring at Uncle Vernon. *"The ghost is settling into him. She's going to hang on, like that girl last night."*

Benedict cringed, remembering the cracking, snapping sounds of her spine.

"Let go, so she can flee into the house again," Emmeline pressed.

"Elys…" Benedict hissed, gaze darting to his brother. He saw his own worries reflected there in the other man's eyes.

"No!" Hazel snapped as though she read their thoughts. God, he hoped she couldn't do that. "Gloria! You will leave this family and this realm! You will go before you harm anyone else!"

Uncle Vernon clicked his teeth in a deliberate, snapping. Drool dribbled thickly off his bottom lip, and his shoulders jerked back in tight spasms.

"Hazel?" Theodore whispered, clutching at his father's hand even as doubt welled in his eyes.

Benedict tried to let go of the hands he held, Luis and Hazel, but they clung to him as though expecting him to be the one who broke first. They had been right.

"Harm. Harm. Harm," the ghost in Uncle Vernon chanted, jerking from side to side with each word. *"Harm. Harm. Harm."*

The walls creaked, and the birds went silent. The paintings and mirrors rattled on the walls, and a *thump* sounded against the center of the table. And then another. Something was knocking.

"Benedict, she's coming," Emmeline warned, her voice strained with worry.

Footsteps beat up and down the halls on the second floor, like someone was searching for something up there— or looking for a way down?

"Benedict!" Emmeline shouted, but it was too late.

The old clock chimed its first cry of midnight, and Uncle Vernon shot to his feet. The birds screamed, wings beating against the cages, shaking them back and forth. The glass in the window frames cracked, and the table lifted off the floor.

Uncle Vernon's mouth dropped open, and he inhaled for what felt like too long, his lungs filling and filling until Benedict was sure they would pop. And then he let out a scream—not his voice at all anymore, but high-pitched and feminine.

Six chimes into midnight, everyone was talking, some commanding Gloria's spirit out while others cried for direction. All seven of their chairs slid back just as the table came crashing down—so heavy that it scored the floor. They finally released one another, Benedict falling backward out of his seat and scrambling on the rug to his feet. The screaming hadn't stopped; it smothered all other sounds.

Eight chimes in and Theodore and Elysium were trying to hold Uncle Vernon against the wall. Hazel chanted, still commanding—still throwing her iron will against the ghost of Gloria Lyon.

"You will pay for what you've done!" the spirit raged from Vernon's throat, somehow without the scream ending, still vibrating through the room. Multiple voices were coming out of Uncle Vernon. The scream, the old man himself groaning beneath, and that furious voice.

Lucy pressed her palms to her ears, backing away from the others and staring.

Ten chimes in and Elysium was suddenly thrown back, off the floor and over the table, into the far wall. His temple whacked against the doorframe, and his body fell limp. Uncle Vernon shoved Theodore off his other arm, tossing his grown son aside. The old man stood straight, no longer crooked. He grinned saliva-slick lips at them all.

Twelve chimes, and the candles went out.

The room sank into darkness, and a second of breathless silence stretched around Benedict, threatening to swallow him in the irrational fear that he would never hear or see again—that everything would be this nerve-wracking nothing forever.

"Get the lights!" Theodore shouted.

Benedict shoved a trembling hand into his pocket and pulled out his lighter, thumbing back the lid.

He heard the frantic flicking of switches, but the lights didn't come on. "It won't work!" Lucy cried.

The room was alive with sounds but no longer the disorienting ones of a spirit's unrest. Panting breaths and shoes scuffing across the floor. Benedict stroked the lighter, bringing that little flame into the room. Within seconds, Theodore had done the same. They hurriedly lit enough candles to push back the shadows.

"Where did he go?" Hazel shouted even though the room had gone quiet. She turned, candle in hand, to study every corner, but Uncle Vernon was gone. "We have to find him. Aunt Gloria's spirit could hurt him…" she continued, stepping over Elysium's unconscious body. She pushed open the doors and disappeared into the hallway.

Benedict cursed her, crouching beside his brother and rolling him onto his back.

"Where's Luis?" Lucy asked, still catching her breath.

He was gone, too. Benedict hadn't seen Luis since the first strokes of midnight. "Maybe he's hiding?" he suggested absently.

Elysium breathed steadily, though he had an ugly cut on his temple. He woke before Benedict got the chance to slap him. A shame. He wasn't sure he would ever get another opportunity to smack his eldest brother without getting the beating of his life for it.

Elysium winced and sat up. "What happened?"

"Uncle Ver—" Lucy started, her words choked off when a gunshot cracked through the house, echoing down from upstairs.

They all jumped, chins tipping up, gazes directed at the ceiling as though they could see through it.

A pained, wailing scream followed, launching them all into motion. They pushed out into the hallway and toward the stairs.

Chapter Thirteen

The flame of Benedict's lighter flared, the brightness of it stretching sideways. He slowed and swayed. The others were moving ahead of him, their footfalls beating at the stairs and against his skull. He winced back, squinting against the straining threads of light pulling at his vision. "What..." he tried, voice heaving out, breath thin. He sucked in hard, trying to fill his lungs, but he couldn't. His heart hammered against his chest and his legs buckled.

He cried out in pain when his knees hit the floor, surprised by the rawness of them. He fell sideways to get his weight off of them, his shoulder pushing against a wall. He pulled his legs up, hand cupping one knee and feeling the wet fabric of his pants. When he pressed at his knee, the pain spiked again, the flesh soft and swollen. He pulled his hand back and squinted down at the blood on his fingers.

It was then he realized he wasn't holding his lighter anymore. He wasn't in the foyer either. He leaned back and looked up. Benedict was inside a closet, and the whole world had gone quiet. No coats were hanging above him, just a bare rod. The door had no handle on the inside, and he knew it was locked—he knew it deep down in his stomach, where fear knotted together in fist-sized panic. Light spilled in from under the door and through the large keyhole. Every breath he dragged in was sharp with the stink of piss, burning his lungs.

A sniffle came from beside him in the little closet, and he snapped his head toward it.

Emmeline crouched there, in the other corner, thighs to her chest and knees scraped open. Her hands pressed against her face, fingers spreading enough to have one eye staring at the door. Tears dripped off her chin, chest rising and falling in fast, panicked breaths that rocked her whole body. "I want to go home," she cried, words muffled into her palms.

Benedict nodded slowly. He wanted to go home, too. That's what they would do. He would get them out of this closet, and they would leave. He didn't care what happened to the Lyon house. He didn't care what they did about his mother's ghost. He and Emmeline would leave.

Voices came from outside the door, familiar but garbled. He leaned up to look through the keyhole. A woman paced out there. He couldn't see her face, but there was something chillingly familiar about how she swung her cigarette back and forth impatiently. Benedict had never seen this place before. There were no windows or doors from the sightline of the keyhole, just a stone table covered with thick candles for light. The woman argued with someone, their voices bouncing back and forth.

Tears blurred his vision, his breath coming out in tighter and tighter gasps. It was her fear, he realized. Emmeline's emotions were *spilling into him.*

"I want to go home," she cried again, and Benedict nodded, understanding now. Not their home. Not the place where they live together in the city with a room just for her, but the place where she had last felt safe before she died. Her mother's house.

Benedict turned and really looked at his best friend in that closet. She wasn't gray like a corpse. She wasn't bloody from knife wounds yet. Her cheeks were flushed, and her knees still oozed blood from where they had been scraped open. She was alive. He reached toward her with a shaking hand, fingertips touching her temple, feeling the heat of her skin pour through his digits. He shuddered a sob when she reached for him, holding on to his arm and the front of his shirt. He cradled one side of her face in his hand, the other battered and swollen. "I want to go home," she pleaded, and he knew he couldn't take her home—not away from this. This wasn't a place. It was a memory.

A shoe scuffed the ground on the other side of the door, and Benedict turned toward it, staring through the keyhole again, but the room was gone, no more light shining through. The key turned in the lock and dread pitched in his heart, just as it had in hers long ago. They both reeled back, suddenly desperate to stay inside, clinging to one another.

Benedict could not untangle his feelings from hers, both hammering through his veins. He held her tight, one hand buried in her hair and his body curling in front of hers, trying to shield her from her fate. Her pain shuddered through him, choking him with terror and misery and a deep, endless pleading for escape.

The door opened, and they both screamed, eyes shut, knowing that there would never be an escape—knowing that there was no going home.

Benedict fell forward, landing on his hands and knees on a rug. He expected pain but felt only the sting of confusion. Sound swirled around him, too many voices shouting in the room. He sat back slowly, blinking at the upstairs library. How had he gotten there? For a second, the shouting ebbed, and his siblings and cousins gawked at him with the same question reflected in their gazes.

"You have to pay!" Uncle Vernon roared, drawing everyone's attention back to him. He paced behind his desk with a revolver in his hand. Elysium, Hazel, and Theodore were crouched behind an overturned table near the door, and Luis was sprawled out on the floor in the center of the room, hands clawing at his stomach around a well of blood. His mouth opened and closed, no longer able to get the screams out like before.

"Mother!" Elysium shouted, glancing sideways at Benedict.

Benedict leaned up on his knees, nearest Uncle Vernon and all the way on the other side of the room. How had he gotten past his uncle and over here?

Elysium stood slowly from behind the table, hands in the air. Hazel pulled at his vest, trying to drag him back down. There were holes in the wood shelter, proof that Uncle Vernon had already fired at least two shots at them. "Mother, I don't know why you're doing this…"

Uncle Vernon shook his head, pacing. *"You know why!"*

"Please!" Elysium called, an edge of panic wheedling into his voice. "If we are guilty, then we will pay at the end, like everyone else. But you never did anything that wasn't for the good of the family. You have nothing to fear about crossing over!"

Benedict crawled toward Luis on the floor, hands pressing over his and against the wet patch on his shirt. Luis groaned and arched, spitting up a mouthful of blood. His eyes rolled back, teeth painted red and mouth gaping.

"You have no idea!" the ghost shouted. *"You think you know what comes next? You think you know how payment will be taken for your crimes? No. We played with something, pretending to be gods. Just because we could see spirits—because we could use our will to push them out of the world—we thought we had the right to do it. It was my duty! My glory! My sin!"*

Elysium shook his head, and Benedict saw the very moment doubt spilled into his brother's heart—like ink splattering a clean page. It had never been there before, but it would never leave him now. "Mother… If this is really you…" he tried, already wanting to pretend this spirit wasn't the same soul that had taught him all his beliefs.

"Oh, it is, boy. And you should know, your will is not stronger than mine. No one can make me go. No one can push me out. And no seal can break me," the ghost swore, and then Uncle Vernon turned the gun on himself, pushing the barrel up against the soft flesh under his chin.

"No!" Elysium screamed, launching forward.

Uncle Vernon, or maybe their mother inside his mind,

stared straight at Elysium when he pulled the trigger. The gun fired, and Uncle Vernon's body snapped back, brains splattering the wall and ceiling. His heavy body collapsed behind his desk with a final *thud*, and Hazel screamed. She pushed off the floor, already in a sprint toward her father.

The house trembled, walls shaking and picture frames falling. Doors opened and slammed up and down the second floor before a terrible thudding ran down the stairs. She was in the house. She was showing them so that Elysium would know the truth of her threats. They could not cast out Gloria Lyon. She was a poltergeist now. This house was hers, and she would not yield it, and no one here had the strength to move her.

"Elys!" Benedict shouted, just as Luis went slack under him, palms still pressing the gunshot wound on his stomach. He looked around for someone else, anyone else, but Hazel rocked her father's corpse in her arms, and Theodore sat on his ass in the doorway, staring at the dead man.

Emmeline lingered in the corner. She wore the same outfit as always, the same as he had seen her wearing in the closet, but she wasn't the same woman. The one in the closet had been alive, full of fear and heartache. The ghost in the corner was still, empty of life, and pulsing with fury.

"Elys!" he tried again, but his brother was already moving to him, dropping to his knees on the other side of Luis's body.

Tears rolled off Elysium's lashes when he held their brother's face, looking into those open, glassy eyes. He felt for a pulse even though they both knew he was gone, and then he pushed at Benedict's shoulder. At first, Benedict couldn't move, couldn't give up the pressure he had been holding on the wound. Elysium patted his chest firmly, pushing him until he finally gave up and sagged back onto the floor.

"What's happening?" Benedict asked.

"You should leave," Elysium whispered, gaze still fixed on Luis. "Go grab your things, Benny. Take the car and go. Just go."

"What are you—"

"Just go," Elysium said again.

Benedict clenched his teeth, wanting to argue just for the sake of arguing—because he didn't want to be told to leave. He wanted to storm out of this house because *he* had decided to go. Maybe he had even wanted Elysium to try to stop him. To give him a speech about family loyalty and convince him to stay.

He looked down at their brother's corpse. He had never been close with Luis—never really wanted to be. And suddenly he regretted that because now he could never change it. He could never take it back or get to know him better.

Their uncle lay on the other side of the desk. How many people had died since he got here? Three? Four?

Benedict pushed himself to his feet, using the wall to brace himself and smearing blood on the surface. He staggered out of the room, stepping over Theodore.

Emmeline joined him in the hallway, walking back to their room in silence.

He opened the door and held it for her.

She slipped past, and for one blissful second, things felt normal. They were together and alone—just the way he liked it.

"Wash your hands before you touch anything…" Emmeline said, the command mild, as though she wouldn't really care if he rubbed his bloody hands clean on the sofa.

He walked to the bathroom, heart hammering in his chest as he replayed everything that had happened from the moment he walked into the parlor for the séance. "Is that really my mother's ghost?"

"Yes. But it isn't her anger." Emmeline followed him to linger in the open door of the bathroom. The habit of leaving doors open for her was so ingrained that he hadn't even thought to do it. He never wanted to close her out.

He turned on the water, smudging the porcelain handle on the sink. He stuck his hands under the cold water, rubbing his brother's blood from his skin. Luis was dead. Uncle Vernon was dead. Mother was dead. And at least two of the staff had been killed.

"Whose anger is it, Emmeline?" he whispered, afraid to know—afraid of having to turn on the one person he'd loved his whole adult life.

"You're going to leave me in this house this time."

He looked up to catch her reflection in the mirror, not the ghost but the living girl from his vision—the one with bruises and tears and so much fear in her eyes. "I won't," he promised.

She forced a smile that only made her appear sadder. His heart cracked. *"You have to. Or you'll die, too, this time."*

He turned around with hands still wet. The ghost stood in his doorway, no tears or bruises or bloodstains. Just his Emmeline, colors muted but for the moving swirls of green in her eyes. "Where is it? That closet you showed me… Where is it?" Benedict pressed.

She cringed, sliding a step back and away from the bathroom door.

He followed her, forgetting to turn off the sink. "Was it close by? Was it in the village by the river? Can you remember?"

"Stop."

He did, both his words and his body halted. He couldn't make her tell him. She might not even know. Ghosts didn't always.

They stared at one another, and he thought about all the versions of her he had known. Sometimes he thought of her as his partner because he was sure he would spend his whole life in her company. She had been a strange burden in the beginning, a curse, and then a friend and a lifeline to faking his way into the family legacy. Somewhere along the way, she had become more important than the legacy. More important than the family.

He turned back to the bathroom, finished cleaning his hands, and then turned off the sink. He changed his clothes, leaving the blood-splattered ones on the floor and dressing in a pair of jeans and a t-shirt. Fuck formality.

Emmeline hugged herself, watching him with pressed lips, like she wasn't sure if she should be angry or guilty. That seemed about right for Emmeline. She was never guilty without a little anger rearing up.

He sighed, staring at his bag after he pulled out a fresh pair of socks. He couldn't look at her when he asked, "Em, is the anger infecting my mother's ghost yours?"

"Yes."

Benedict nodded once, pulled on his sockets and his shoes, and then grabbed his bag. "Let's go home." If he took her away from this place, maybe his mother would settle down and Elysium could convince her to move on. At the very least, maybe she would stop slaughtering everyone inside.

Chapter Fourteen

Benedict dropped his bag beside the front door, staring out at what he had already heard. A summer storm was passing over the property, pelting the house with heavy drops of rain that appeared as a haze outside, obscuring the tree line into a smear of distant greens. The dirt roads were thick puddles fast bleeding into one another, creating a shallow river, and the whole house sang with the sound of rain beating at the rooftop and rattling the old windows in their frames.

Elysium met him at the entrance, his shirt and vest soaked through and dark hair sticking to his cheek. "The tires have been slashed on all of the cars. All of them. Even the spares," he said.

Benedict's brow pinched. "How is that possible?"

"We can't find Lucy..." Theodore reported, winded and standing in the foyer behind them. "She vanished sometime after the séance and before dad..." His jaw twitched, tears welling unbidden in his eyes. He looked up, as though he could stub out his own sadness. "I checked the whole house, but I can't find her."

"You think she's possessed?" Elysium asked.

"I don't know," Theodore said quickly. "Maybe she made a run for it?"

"And slashed all the tires before leaving?" Benedict pressed. He glanced around, looking for Emmeline, but he hadn't seen her since he left his room.

"Maybe."

"Can we call someone then?" Benedict asked, though he suspected he already knew the answer. And he couldn't exactly drive out on the rims in the mud.

"The house line is dead, and we're not getting service. I think the storm is interfering," Elysium said grimly. They had never gotten particularly good wireless connections out here on the estate, and Mother hadn't minded. She preferred calls to the old house phone.

"What are we going to do now?" Theodore asked, impatient. "The sun is coming up. We need to figure something out before night."

Benedict turned, staring at his cousin. Since when was he afraid of the dark?

Theodore clicked his teeth angrily at him, seeming to hear the accusation. "Everything got worse when the clock struck midnight. And the night before—when that maid killed the footman and then herself—that was after midnight, too."

From the way Elysium straightened, it seemed Benedict hadn't been the only one not to think of the timing.

"If we don't think of something soon, I'm going to start walking," Theodore said.

"It might not be the worst idea..." Benedict agreed.

"And just give up the house to a ghost?" Hazel snapped from the staircase. All three men turned to look up at her. Her hair was still wet from a shower. Last time Benedict had seen her, she'd been clinging to her father's corpse, his blood pouring out over her hands and dripping onto the floor. "No. This is our house."

Theodore barked a laugh at his sister. "Who gives a shit about the house, Hazel? I'll buy you another one!"

Hazel ignored him, the furious patter of the storm still rolling in thick and humid through the open front doors. She glared down at Elysium. "Are you really going to leave your mother to haunt this place? For how long?"

Elysium weighed her with his dark gaze, appearing unconvinced.

"And Luis's body? My father's? Will you leave them in the kitchen to rot?"

Elysium cringed. "We'll come back for them."

"Bullshit," Hazel snapped. "You know you can't just walk out of here. There are miles of woods between you and the road and a poltergeist in this house. Are you willing to bet she can't follow you to the edge of the estate?"

Theodore swore and began to pace, much like his father used to. "That's absurd..."

"All of this is absurd!" Hazel yelled. "But we have a

job to do. We can cleanse this house and put our dead to rest."

"This isn't the time to play leader of the pack," Theodore muttered bitterly.

Hazel ignored her brother, still staring hard at Elysium. "Gloria would not have run from her own house."

Benedict laughed then, surprising them all. "No. She wouldn't. Which is exactly why Elysium is trying to get us out of here. I am not stupid enough to think that I can force her out of this house, especially not now that she's gone poltergeist."

"Of course, *you* can't," Hazel raked her gaze over him, lip curling. "You didn't even have the sight, let alone any gifts—"

"Stop it," Elysium warned.

She rolled her eyes and looked away. "We have to put them to rest. We can't just run away."

"And are you going to be the one digging a grave in a downpour? Or maybe you'd like to build a pyre?" Theodore's voice rose as he spoke, one long arm sweeping toward the open doors to gesture at the storm outside and the morning darkened by the curtains of rain.

The floorboards creaked down the length of the foyer, dragging all of their attention into the shadows at the far end. Lucy shifted from one foot to the other. A puddle of mud grew around her, water dripping off her dress, her sleeves, and her curls.

"Lucy?" Elysium called, catching Theodore's elbow before he could walk toward her. They studied her for seconds that felt drawn out into minutes before relaxing all at once. Benedict understood why—they had used their sight to search for a ghost possessing her and found none. Benedict pretended to have come to the same conclusion.

"It's her..." Lucy mumbled, making no move to come closer.

As a group, they inched toward her. She held her hands out in front of herself, staring at them. Her arms were gloved in mud, nails broken, and hands swollen and bloody.

"Where have you been?" Hazel asked.

"Did you slash the tires?" Theodore demanded.

Lucy continued to stare at her hands, brows pushing toward the middle of her face as though she didn't recognize the palms and dirty fingers. "It's her," she said again, dazed.

"Who?" Elysium asked. "Mother?"

Tears gathered in her dark eyes, making them shimmer when she shook her head.

"Where were you?" Benedict tried. It seemed that asking questions was the thing to do.

Lucy let out a wobbling breath. "I don't remember going to the graveyard... I don't remember digging her up but..."

"You dug up your mother?" Hazel almost shrieked.

Elysium gestured his cousin away and cautiously stepped up to his sister's side, taking her by the wrist with one hand while the other braced her back. "Let's get you cleaned up."

Lucy took a couple of steps, lulled into his care before jumping to life and twisting from his hold. She shook her head. "No! We have to get out of here!"

"You kind of made that impossible..." Hazel muttered. It seemed she had decided to lay the blame for the slashed tires and cut phone line on Lucy. She was probably right. It seemed Lucy had lost herself for a while and ended up in the graveyard. There was no knowing for certain what she had or hadn't done. But Benedict shot Hazel a glare anyway. She was being particularly heartless, and none of them deserved it.

"She's coming for us. It's her!" Lucy continued to wail.

Theodore made shushing sounds and gently took her arms, replacing Elysium. "We know. We know your mother is—"

"No!" Lucy wailed, body shaking so hard that she had to lean into Theodore to keep from crumbling to the floor. "Not Mother." Her gaze slashed to Benedict, sending a chill down his spine. She repeated, "*Her.*"

Elysium and Theodore exchanged looks, as though this meant something to them. Her. Not Mother. But *her.*

"She's lost her mind," Hazel whispered, but the fire had gone from her words.

"Get her upstairs," Elysium told Theodore hurriedly. "She needs to rest. We'll figure out what to do."

"No! No. She's coming for us!" Lucy continued to cry as Theodore all but carried her up the stairs. "We have to pay! She's going to make us pay!"

The three of them stood in the foyer until it fell quiet again, as quiet as it could be with the roar of a storm still pouring in.

"Who?" Benedict demanded before anyone could say anything else.

"No one." Hazel found her voice. "Your mother obviously possessed Lucy to keep us in this house."

"Convenient for you," Elysium added.

"Why does Lucy think she's guilty? Guilty of what?" Benedict pressed, not letting them change the subject.

"Nothing!" Hazel shouted. "I didn't do anything wrong, and I don't deserve this. I have only ever protected this family and—"

"Now who's the one possessed by Mother?" Benedict interrupted. "You're practically quoting her."

"Benny…" Elysium tried, his voice back to that careful, even tone, but when Benedict turned toward him, he saw uncertainty in those eyes. It hadn't been there before last night.

"What is she talking about? *Who* is she talking about?"

For one thrilling second, Benedict actually thought Elysium would tell him whatever the great secret was— that he would come clean and lay everything bare. And then Elysium pressed his lips shut and shook his head once, looking away like a king dismissing a subject.

Benedict almost stayed, just to be willful. Almost took a big step forward and shoved Elysium back.

But he didn't. He remembered the mud all over Lucy

and her rambling about the graveyard. She had woken up out there from whatever trance possessed her. Mother's ghost had released her after she dug up her grave. Why? No one was going to answer him, that was painfully clear. So, Benedict turned and stomped down the hallway.

He wanted to call for Emmeline. He wanted her to tell him all the secrets of his home the way she had told him the secrets in other haunted houses. She had been his eyes everywhere they went. Why wasn't she that way here? The few days since they arrived felt like weeks. She had been distant and strange the whole time. Maybe he got it wrong? Maybe it wasn't Emmeline infecting the house—maybe the house was infecting Emmeline?

He passed the dining room and turned down the narrow hallway to the back of the house. The floor was muddy here, too, Lucy's wet footprints leading in from the storm. She had left the backdoor open, swinging on its hinges, caught in a warm breeze that bounced it on the wall.

"Benedict!" Elysium called after him, voice echoing down the hall just before he stepped out into the storm.

The fury of the warm rain muffled his brother's voice. The sopping ground sank under his steps, soaking into his boots. He was drenched before he had gone a dozen steps from the house, but he kept walking even when the rain rolled freely down his face in constant rivulets, spilling off his chin.

If he weren't soaked from the rain, he would have been soaked from sweat by the time he reached the graveyard, the oppressive heat of the rising morning made brutally muggy by the storm. Each breath he sucked was wet heat sticking in his lungs.

Elysium stopped calling him. He didn't follow. Why would he? What could he do now? Drag Benedict back into the house? Keep him captive? To what end?

Benedict used his whole hand to scrub the rain from his face, trying to clear his vision long enough to get a look at the muddy yard. He stood in front of the fresh mound of his mother's grave. The rain had made it flat, puddling on top of it where even this soft ground wasn't fast enough to drink up the downpour. No one had dug her up. Nothing was out of place.

He glanced around at the others, old stones and trimmed grass patches—just as they had been before.

His stomach knotted and the muscles in his legs ached, threatening to give out on him. He turned toward the woods, toward that spot where Emmeline had sat during the funeral— staring at the ground.

He forced himself to take those last steps, legs shaking and breaths coming in heaving gasps.

The little hole in the ground was full of rainwater. It wasn't cleanly shaped by a shovel or a spade. No. Lucy had clawed up the grass and flowers and used her arms to scoop away the mud and rocks, making a little mound to the side.

Benedict crouched over it, staring at the well of murky water. He reached in with both hands and pulled out the muddy bundle at its depths. He held it for a long while, heart hammering in his chest. He didn't want to open it. He didn't want whatever this gift was. But he needed it.

He laid it on the grass and plucked at the thick strings used to bind the package. His hands shook.

It was his mother's work. He had seen her put the last possessions of the dead to rest before. It was her way of paying respect and offering peace. It was the greatest kindness she could ever have been bothered to offer, and it was because she knew—*knew*—that there could be real consequences for leaving a spirit unsettled.

He pulled at the fabric caked in mud and plastered to itself in layers. The rain helped, washing his hands every time they lifted from the muddy flaps and finally rinsing off the items exposed. His stomach twisted, threatening to heave.

A pair of women's black boots. They were well worn, the sole of one even had a little hole in it.

Tears ran with the rain down his cheeks.

He knew these shoes, didn't he? How many times had he bought a pair just like them for Emmeline?

Someone stepped into the edge of his vision, and he forced his gaze to slide up, a cry choking in his throat when he saw her standing there—his Emmeline. His best friend. The love of his life. The rain cut through her, gray skin dewy in sweat and smeared in blood. The front of her dress stuck to her belly, holes glinting darkest with blood that bloomed outward into macabre flowers, saturating the thin fabric. The rain, here and now, did nothing to wash away the blood from long ago. Nothing could wash it away. Nothing could change what had been done.

He counted the crimson flowers as they grew, appearing one after the other, clustered against her abdomen. Seven. Seven stab wounds.

Her hands were broken, and her wrists bruised from the ropes. One side of her face swelled as he stared at her, an eye pressing closed while the other, vicious in that brilliant green, called for vengeance.

He heard that call now—clear as a bell.

She had been calling to him all these years with those eyes, with that look and the glimpses of silent, haunted misery. Because that was the true darkness of ghosts—not how the living imagined themselves to be haunted, but that the ghosts were the ones being chased and choked by regret, pain, and rage.

Emmeline's broken lips pulled into the smallest of tired smiles he had ever witnessed, and his heart crumbled right there in his chest. She stared at the shoes in front of him like long-lost friends.

And suddenly his ghost wasn't barefoot anymore.

After nine years, she had found her shoes.

Chapter Fifteen

"Tell me," Benedict said to her as they stood in the rain.

Emmeline stared. *"I have been."*

He carried the boots back to the house. Maybe she couldn't say it with words. Was that why he had been seeing visions? He knew now, without a doubt, that Emmeline had ignited his mother's spirit into her current fury. He could feel that anger himself, coiling in his chest, twisting around his heart. He felt Emmeline in a way he never quite had before, but he was certain that it had always been there.

The first days he ever saw her, crouched and sobbing in his bedroom upstairs, her eyes had burned that electric green. He had been terrified of her—of the ghastly appearance of her and all her wild emotions. Somehow, he had gotten used to them, put them aside as something normal for a ghost. But what did he know of ghosts? He only knew Emmeline and the stories of others.

Elysium waited for him at the back door. His eyes flickered from the dirty, old boots hanging from Benedict's hand, back up to his face.

"Why are her shoes here?" Benedict asked the first question he could get out, tears still in his eyes. He stepped out of the storm and into the house, and Elysium stepped back to give him space.

"Whose?" Elysium asked, the word quiet as though he didn't even want to say it.

Benedict smiled furiously and put the shoes down on the narrow table along the wall, puddling mud beside a vase of silk flowers. "Emmeline," he said her name to his brother for the first time.

She came to stand beside them, hand hovering over her lost shoes with wonder.

Elysium's eyes widened. "How do you know that name?"

"How do *you*?" he growled.

"Did someone say it to you? Have you communicated with Mother's spi—"

"I don't communicate with spirits," Benedict cut him off. He had held on to that secret for so long. He had been sure he would keep the truth to himself until the day he died. "I only see one. I only hear one."

Elysium gaped. "Benny…"

"What happened? How did her shoes end up here? Where is the rest of her?" The last sentence came out strangled. He felt Emmeline then, her focus on them and her ghost at his side. Her anger was body heat now, soaking into his arm, spreading through his chest.

"That's not possible. You can't see her. You can't. We put her to rest, Benny. We've never seen her—none of us. Mother would have—"

"I see her." Tears rolled down his rain-soaked cheeks. "How can you not feel her, Elys?" His fingers twisted in the front of his own shirt, pushing hard against his chest. "I can feel her heart breaking. I can feel the knife."

Elysium jerked back, shoulder hitting the wall. His head shook slowly, still trying to resist believing in what he himself could not see. "Benny… I think Mother has—"

"It has nothing to do with her now!" Benedict yelled.

"Ask him again," Emmeline pressed. *"Ask him where I am. Where's my body?"*

"You really see her?" Elysium whispered, voice trembling in a way Benedict had never heard before.

"Yes," he glanced to the side. Emmeline balled her hands into fists against her waist. "Who did it? Who killed her? Why?" He had so many questions—though none of them seemed to be the ones Emmeline cared about.

A thunder of steps barreled down the staircase, Theodore chasing Hazel into the foyer down the hall. They spilled into their line of sight just as Theo caught his sister by the elbow and jerked her to a stop. "Lucy swears she's still here. We have to at least consider—"

"No!" Hazel yelled. "It is just Gloria trying to torture us."

"Why?" Theodore matched her volume. "Why would

she do that?"

"Because she was a crazy bitch—"

"Why dig up the dead girl's shoes?" he hissed in a whisper, obviously not meant for Benedict to hear. So they knew about Emmeline, too? Had they all known? Was that why Lucy had been so quick to press Mother's ghost out of that maid? Was she worried about her giving away the secret?

"What did you do?" Benedict heaved the words, turning his gaze to his brother across from him in the dark hall.

Hazel and Theodore continued to argue in the foyer.

Elysium swallowed hard; something caught in his throat, maybe? He reached for Benedict. Why? They had never been the hugging sort, and no firm handshake was going to fix this. "Nothing. We didn't do anything."

"Liar," Emmeline hissed bitterly.

"Liar," Benedict repeated, because it should be heard by more than just himself. All these years, Emmeline had been holding on to that rage. It had been spilling out here and there, and like a fool, he had assumed it was just a part of being a ghost. He had set aside her feelings as a dramatic consequence of lingering. He had ignored her broken heart, her broken body, and her need to have that fury heard.

He grabbed the boots off the table and walked straight down the hall.

Hazel and Theodore choked on their argument at the sight of him. Theodore reeled back when he spotted the old shoes from the pitiful little grave. Neither said anything to him, just stared. Benedict took the stairs two at a time, and before he reached the second floor, they were back to bickering over their fleeting options, Elysium's deep voice joining them in a conspiratorial whisper.

Instead of going to his room to seek solitude or refuge like he had as a teen—the last time he had been in this house—he swung right at the intersection of halls and went straight for Lucy's room. For the first time in his life, he didn't knock.

Her room had the same layout as his, a little parlor in the front leading through an archway into the bedroom with her own bathroom and closet. She jumped when the door slammed against the wall, leaping off the dark satin couch. Everything in her room was in mauve, wine red, and black, with a theme of skulls and Ouija board trinkets she had collected since she was a teen. She leaned Goth long before she left home to build a following of tarot readers and séance holders. She dropped her teacup when she saw the boots, fresh tears gathering in her already swollen eyes. "No. No."

He thumped them down on her coffee table. "Who did it?"

"We're past that," Emmeline whispered, but he wasn't.

Her hands, freshly bandaged, hovered in the air between her chest and her mouth—not sure where to go, he supposed. "No. I… No."

"Lucy." He said her name firmly, and her gaze snapped from the shoes to him. "Tell me why we're all going to die in this house tonight."

Some of her tears spilled over, but her mouth pulled

into a desperate smile. "We did something terrible. Mother said it was okay. She said it wouldn't matter because it was for a good reason, and she…she…she…" Lucy got stuck on the word.

"Me," Emmeline hissed at her, hovering over the other woman but going unseen. *"Me. Me. Me."*

"She wouldn't be missed," Lucy hiccupped. "Mother said. It was for a good cause, and it would give her life purpose. Really… Really, we were saving her from a tragic life and—"

"Saving her?" Benedict almost threw up, gagging on the words.

Lucy lunged at him, kicking her forgotten teacup on the floor and fumbling to latch onto his hand with her tender, gauze-gloved ones. "I swear, Benny! She was no one. A broken family and a dark future!"

"My broken family!" Emmeline screamed. *"My future!"*

He tore his hand from his sister's hold and staggered back. "You were part of it? You killed her?"

Lucy choked on a sob. "We needed a sacrifice, Benny! It wasn't *killing.* We were just moving her on to the next life. It was a mercy. She would have had a hard life."

Emmeline screamed, and Benedict winced, hands flying to his ears.

Lucy cried harder, probably thinking that he was trying not to hear her excuses. "It had to be done! We were saving you!" she pleaded.

The tall windows in her bedroom that overlooked the

front of the house rattled in their frames.

Lucy whirled around, eyes bulging, but she wouldn't see anything, would she? This wasn't Mother shaking the room with her wrathful screams. This was Emmeline. His Emmeline.

The windows cracked, and with the pitch of that cry only he could hear, they burst, spraying glass inside rather than out.

Lucy screamed and twisted away from the explosion, panting for air. Her arms trembled, bent up to shield the sides of her face. "It really is her, isn't it? She really is still here?" she whispered.

Benedict staggered back, struggling to catch his breath in the wake of Emmeline's flash of anger. "Yes. She's always been with me."

Lucy let out a string of mad laughs tangled with cries. "We thought we sent her on. We didn't know… It was supposed to give you her sight so that you could see the spirit world like the rest of us. We made her a ghost so that you could see like a ghost, but it was only supposed to keep her sight. Not her." She sank to her knees, clutching at her head. "Not her."

Benedict backed out of the room, shoulder hitting the doorframe.

Emmeline bent over Lucy, her hands balled against her bloody skirt and jaw dropping open wide to let loose another furious scream right in Lucy's face, but she didn't see. She didn't even hear it. But she felt the tremble of the room.

She gasped when the glass shards lifted off the floor, making gentle sounds in the air before flinging at her in a vicious rush.

A part of him thought to save her. She was his sister, after all. But she had done this, hadn't she? She had purchased this pain. Wasn't it right that she knelt before it now?

He turned, groping at the doorknob. Emmeline's scream was too much; it pressed at his skull and rang against his eardrums. His stomach lurched, his whole body pushing forward as though to outrun the return of his last meal. He all but fell out the door, the rug seeming to slide under his shoes.

Benedict squeezed his eyes shut and breathed, trying not to vomit. Sweat clung to his skin, clothes still wet from the storm outside.

He realized too late that the screaming had stopped. He couldn't even hear Lucy crying.

He straightened slowly, blinking against the sudden darkness. Thick candles flickered along the wall. No. It couldn't be night already.

Shadows moved in the room, voices far away and growing closer. This wasn't the hallway or any bedroom he was familiar with. The shadows took shape, silhouettes slipping out to become people gathering around a table without chairs.

He shivered, cold despite the summer heat he had been bathed in only seconds ago. He recognized this room from a keyhole.

"Are you certain?" Elysium asked, and it sounded like the hundredth time, his voice tight and a little angry.

Benedict blinked at his brother, his hair a little longer and his clothes not quite as fitted. He was younger, maybe the same age as Benedict. He remembered when his hair had been that length. He had cut it not long after Benedict moved out of the house to go to school.

"Enough," Gloria snapped at him. "If you don't want to do it, then take her home."

Elysium cringed, fists pressed to his thighs but no longer arguing.

Benedict stared, stepping closer as his mother took a deep drag from her cigarette.

The dark room filled with shadows taking shape. Luis hovered close to their mother's side, and Hazel whispered to Uncle Vernon. Theodore had his arms crossed firmly against his chest. He wasn't as well dressed as the man he would become, hair a mess and sweater hanging on his thin frame. Lucy, like the rest of them, was younger, but much the same as always. She chewed her lower lip, the way she did when nervous. They all looked guilty; the weight of it sapping their youth right before his eyes.

"Get on with it," Gloria ordered.

Elysium hesitated.

Benedict couldn't remember ever seeing his brother hesitate when it came to commands from their mother. But, at last, he disappeared from the gathering of somber faces around that table.

Benedict wanted to follow him, he tried to, but he couldn't seem to find the edges of the room, the scene became foggy beyond the table and no matter how he walked, he couldn't get far from it.

A scream pierced the room, and he spun toward his family just in time to catch the grimaces of his siblings and cousins.

Elysium returned, carrying Emmeline in his arms. She kicked and struggled as best she could with her wrist and ankles bound. She cried, clawing at his shoulder with broken fingers and begged him to let her go. His dark eyes fixed on the table; Elysium wouldn't look at her. He lifted her and put her on the surface. Their mother was quick to grab the tail of rope trailing Emmeline's wrists, dragging it back and flattening the girl out on the surface, tying her arms to the edge of the table over her head.

She sobbed, struggling to drag in enough air to scream. Her heels kicked at the table, thunking again and again, her whole body spasming in terror.

Benedict tried to push his way into the circle of his relatives, but he fell through them. "Stop!" he commanded, but they didn't hear him. He reached for her on the table, desperate to pick her up and run away, but his hands passed right through her and his heart sank low into his stomach. He gasped wildly for air, her sobs endless and his joining hers. He was the ghost now—trespassing on a scene of the living past.

Uncle Vernon handed his mother that old, leather-bound notebook from the witch's house—the one he had seen as a boy and never again since. Mother had called it hokum, but she flipped it open now. She was rough with the pages as though offended by them even as she read the scribbles of spells and madness they had to offer.

"Please, please let me go," Emmeline tried, her voice so raw that it didn't even sound like her anymore. "I won't tell. I just want to go home!" Her words pitched with terror, cracking in her throat.

They ignored her—already a ghost to them.

"We gather tonight to offer this vessel," his mother announced.

"Carry her to the next world and leave the sight of spirits in our care. We will it."

"We will it," the other six repeated.

Benedict shuddered. Why?

"Please!" Emmeline wailed.

Lucy cried silently, and Theodore stared hard at the edge of the table.

"Leave us the gifts of souls, the gifts of this spirit, and bless them on our boy, Benedict."

"Benedict," they repeated.

Tears rolled hotly down his cheeks. He wanted to scream—the way Emmeline's ghost had screamed with waves of mind-shattering fury and pain, but it caught in his throat, strangling him.

Somewhere far away, upstairs, the old clock chimed the first bells of midnight.

They passed around a knife, and he watched, helpless against the past, as those closest to him took turns stabbing her. Seven wounds. One at a time. Her screams grew louder and louder until the last one came in a wheeze, her breath hitching in her lungs and that one eye, the one not swollen shut, bulging. She arched off the table, mouth open wide but getting no air, only gurgling up blood like a slow fountain.

Benedict's legs gave out.

She died.

He heaved forward and vomited.

Chapter Sixteen

Benedict vomited violently, hurling up everything in his stomach and then heaving breathlessly. His vision blurred, and his throat burned, coated in stomach acid. He coughed and fell back, gasping for air and sobbing.

A hand pressed against his shoulder, firm and real. "Benny?" Elysium asked, worry thick in his voice. "Are you okay? Where did you come from?"

Benedict jerked away from him, shoving at his brother's chest. He needed space. He needed to catch his breath.

Benedict let out a miserable groan. He was still in the same room, only the fog at the edges had receded to expose old stone walls and a dirt floor under his ass. He blinked up at them, his murderous family—or what was left of them, anyway.

Hazel, Theodore, and Elysium had gathered around that table, the witch's journal laid out on it with a battery-powered lantern beside it, stretching light through the room. It smelled like a grave. How had he never realized they had a basement before? How had he never realized they were killers?

"You murdered her," he said once he caught his breath, tears still blurring his vision, hanging on his bottom lashes.

"*Jesus*," Theodore hissed. "She really is here…"

Elysium didn't grab at him again, but he squatted down to get at eye level. It wasn't unlike the way he had squatted beside him as a boy, when Benedict would fall down or find himself in a fit of terror—there had been much to be frightened of in this house as a kid. Elysium would always be the calming voice of reason, laying things out for him just as they are but with the added promise that he would be okay. And Benedict had always believed him, even in the thick of their worst fights, he had believed Elysium.

"How did you get down here? You weren't here before, and there's only one door," he nudged his head in the direction of an old wooden staircase. "Benny, you weren't here, and then you suddenly were."

Benedict laughed, startling himself with the sound. "You're disturbed because you don't know how I did it? That's what your takeaway is?"

"Benny—" Elysium tried again, voice ever firm.

"The house moved me," Benedict interrupted him, staring hard to see the traces of fear swirling deep in those eyes—eyes like his own. "I saw it. I saw what you did. I know why you're going to die here tonight—why we're all going to die."

Hazel hissed between her teeth. "Fuck that," she snapped.

"I am not going to be killed by some nobody ghost."

Benedict sat back, palms pressed into the dirty floor to prop himself up. He tossed his head to the side to look around his brother at his cousins hovering over the table. Theodore looked appropriately terrified, but Hazel still clung to her anger. It had become her buoy in the cold, dark ocean of coming death. "Nobody?" Benedict repeated. "*Your victim*, Hazel. Your victim—or maybe Gloria Lyon herself."

Hazel snorted angrily and flipped through the pages of the notebook. By the furious way she slapped the pages down, one after the other, it seemed it wasn't the first time she had gone through the journal. No spells to undo a murder? No way to take back what they had done?

"Why?" Benedict asked, throat drying around the question and tear-swollen eyes shifting back to Elysium.

His brother still crouched beside him, but his gaze focused on nothing, the way it did when he tried to think his way out of a corner. "What?" he asked distantly before blinking back to the present, brow pinching when he stared at Benedict. "*Why*, what?"

"Why did you kill her? *Why her?*"

Elysium sighed, the way a man does when a piece of his soul leaves his body. "You really see her?"

"Every day."

Elysium nodded slowly, shoulders sagging as much as a person with good posture ever could. "Is she here now?"

"Not in this room." Benedict didn't have to look around to know. He always knew when she was with him. He felt her even when she wasn't, like a line connected them. Was that what they had done? Connected them?

"I'm so sorry," Elysium whispered. "We only meant to give you the sight—*her* sight."

His face burned, the muscles in his jaw jumping when he clamped his teeth together. "You killed her for that? So that I would see ghosts like you?"

"Like all Lyons, Benedict. All of us see them. Uncle Vernon and Mother said that if you couldn't see them—if you didn't develop any gifts—that you would have to be removed from the family line. It's an old tradition, Benny. I tried to talk them out of it, but they said we were all bound by the laws of the Lyon family."

"So what?" he snapped, sitting upright. "So, I would have been kicked out? I left anyway!"

He was halfway to his feet when Elysium said in a quiet voice, "Not kicked out. *Removed.*"

Benedict froze just as his legs straightened. Elysium rose to his feet. He was taller than Benedict, just a little bit, but forever now that they were far from the age of growing. "They were going to kill me?"

Elysium nodded slowly. "It was this or lose you."

All of his air gushed out of him, pushing him a step back. "You're all insane."

"We thought we'd put her to rest, Benny, I swear," Elysium continued. "We thought the spell would leave you with the sight of spirits... We didn't realize it would leave her bound to you for that sight." He spoke carefully, slowly, as though examining something truly baffling.

Benedict burst, body thrusting forward. The heels of his palms slammed into his brother's chest, shoving Elysium back three steps. His ass hit the heavy slab of a table where they had killed Emmeline.

"That's not the point, you shitbag!" Benedict roared. "How can you still not see that what happened, *how it went wrong,* isn't the point? You murdered a girl!"

Theodore stared at him, too, now, eyes big as saucers and body still as a statue. "She was nobody," he whispered. "She would have had a tragic life. We were saving her…" he trailed the same sentiment as Lucy but with even less conviction. It was like the way a child held up a blanket, believing it would hold back all the monsters of the night.

Benedict twisted his face, glaring at his cousin before swinging his attention back to Elysium. "What is that about? Why do they keep saying that?"

"Because that's what we told them," Elysium said quietly. His tone was strange now, gentle, and missing something that had always been there. "Do you remember how sick you were? Your fever?"

Benedict's brow was pinched so tight that his head hurt. "Yeah, sure."

"You were eighteen. They had started poisoning you."

Hazel slammed the old journal shut and shrieked another curse before storming across the room and up the stairs.

Theodore remained, breathing in tight gasps.

"I had to find someone fast," Elysium continued, voice still off—hushed and a little hollow. He had lost his certainty, his firm authority. He was confessing. "Mother would grant you more time if I could find someone for the binding spell—time to see if it worked. So, I found her, and I told them she had no one in her life, a drug addict spiraling toward a fast and tragic end."

Benedict's throat burned with all the screams he swallowed down. "But the truth?"

Elysium lifted his gaze from a spot on the floor, tears swimming in his eyes, but he fought to hold them back. "She wasn't well off. She wasn't going anywhere in life."

"But?"

"She had a family—parents and siblings and friends. She was happy, I think. I don't know. I only saw her a couple of times."

"Why her?" he whispered the question that clawed at his heart.

"She had the same birth date as you. The journal said the trade needed to be as similar as possible. She had the same birth date as you, and she only lived one state over. Uncle Vernon and I grabbed her walking home and drove her here."

Benedict just stared—gawked, really. He'd said it so matter-of-factly.

It had happened, and it was done.

But it wasn't done.

"Mother gave you another year after the ritual to show ability, and you did! I was saving you, Benny," he said, and the authority was back, the vague, almost-apology over. "And I *will* save you. I'll find a way to fix this."

"Fix it?"

"Her ghost is latched on to you, her soul entwined with yours like the roots of two teeth knotted together. That's why you see her and we don't. She'd gone from the world except for what's wrapped around you. You are her only tether."

"Where's her body?" Benedict asked absently, remembering that she had wanted to know.

"Cremated and scattered," Elysium said, brushing aside useless facts. He had already explained that her tether was Benedict, after all.

Benedict took a step back and then another. He glanced past his brother's chair, to Theodore still standing on the other side of the killing table. He cried, shaking his head slowly in that mad way people did when they just couldn't handle reality. They had all seen it in others—in people with ghosts in their homes or spirits trailing them through life.

Good, Benedict thought. *They should feel what it was like to be on the other side of it—on the out-of-control, terrified end of things.*

"Benedict?" Elysium looked up from his thoughts.

His heel bumped the stairs. "I hope you die," he hissed before turning his back on them both. He took the stairs two at a time and pushed the flat door open at the top. He stumbled out into the hallway from a wall panel he had never known was a door.

He dragged two muggy breaths into his lungs and then pivoted toward the foyer. He walked fast, Elysium still calling after him, starting up the stairs himself.

"Where were you?" Emmeline's voice rushed in panic, meeting him in the hallway near the front door. *"I couldn't find you anywhere."*

She hadn't been down there. Maybe she couldn't? It was for the best. "We're leaving," he said. He would have taken her hand if he could.

Emmeline walked at his side, craning to look up at him. *"How? The cars are wrecked, aren't they?"*

Benedict opened the door, holding it for her. "We'll walk. I don't care if we sleep in the woods, we're leaving. Now."

She nodded, and he followed her outside onto the porch. The storm had dwindled to a steady drizzle. If it had been a monsoon, he still would have gone. They were going to try to get rid of Emmeline—it was the only way to save themselves now. Maybe if her spirit were gone, Mother's would settle.

He was down the steps and onto the driveway when something larger than a raindrop hit the ground to his right. He glanced at it before actually stopping. A shoe. One of Emmeline's boots.

"I'm sorry," Emmeline said, just over the rain. He looked at her, suddenly standing not far from the shoe. It was the

sort of sorry a parent says to a child when something inevitable is about to happen—something that they wouldn't stop even if they could—something they might even have decided to do. Like moving, or getting a shot, or having a bone set.

She wasn't looking at the boot on the ground. Emmeline stared up at the house.

His stomach sank deep. He already knew. He knew because she knew.

Still, Benedict twisted back to look up at his childhood home. His sister slid off the ledge of her window. It wouldn't have been far enough to kill her, if she hadn't tipped headfirst toward the ground, arms hugging the other boot.

He barely had the time to brace himself, to register what was happening, and then he watched, unblinking, as Lucy landed, body crumbling in on itself and bending in all the wrong ways. Her spine snapped; he heard it and he recognized it because it wasn't the first time he had heard that sound this weekend.

Lucy had been a beautiful person, but she had not made for a beautiful corpse.

He wrapped his anger around himself like armor and turned his back on her body, walking down the drive until he could slip off it and into the woods. He didn't worry about his red shirt tempting wolves today—he was pretty sure he had been living with them all along.

Chapter Seventeen

They hadn't made it far, maybe twenty minutes into the thick of wet trees before he felt a physical tug at his heart.

Benedict and Emmeline both stopped, hands flying to their chests to press over aching hearts. They exchanged glances. She felt it, too. Something was wrong. Cold fingers ran up his spine, despite the sticky heat of the day.

"What is that?" Benedict whispered. He could almost hear something. A voice? A cry?

Emmeline pivoted back in the direction of the house, staring though it was lost behind the tangled growth of trees and thick bushes. They had been cutting a straight line for the road. He knew this estate well enough to find his way. They would figure out what to do once they got to the pavement.

"I told you we wouldn't survive this place," she whispered.

"What do you mean?"

"They're killing us."

Us. He loved the way it sounded, like they were one person. He supposed, if Elysium was right, they were in some sense one person—their souls knotted up. He realized then what she was saying and turned to follow her gaze through the trees. He remembered that possessed maid the other night. When Lucy had tried to cast out Mother's spirit, it had killed the maid. Would they try to cast Emmeline out? Would he snap like that woman had? One vertebra at a time?

Emmeline took two steps closer to him, close enough that she could reach out and touch him if she weren't spectral. *"Do you want me to stop them?"*

The question stunned him. Could she stop them? Could she simply whisk herself back to the house and… Do what? Agitate his mother's spirit into action? Would she do it herself? Possess someone?

"Do you hate me?" Benedict asked instead of answering. He could feel the imminent danger of time now—the sense of an ax hanging over his head. If he didn't ask now, he might never have a chance.

Emmeline considered him carefully, and he studied the wealth of emotions twisting behind her eyes like a bed of snakes. *"Sometimes,"* she said, and he understood. She did hate him. But she also loved him. He felt it, warming his heart and pushing his spine straight and chin up. Her love made him proud. It had been his source of contentment for years now.

"You know then? That they killed you for me? That it's because of me?" he continued, words almost pushing onto one another in the rush to be spoken. Think if he were to die in the middle? Choked off mid-sentence by his own cracking back.

"Yes," she answered quickly. *"Sometimes the details are foggy, but I always knew it was because of you."*

"When the ghosts would attack me—when we would cleanse houses—was that because of you? Did you want them to kill me?"

"I didn't tell them to do it, but they could feel the part of me that wants you to pay and wants to be free."

"And the other part?"

She smiled suddenly, as though he had told a joke and she couldn't help herself. She stepped closer to him, tears in her eyes. *"The other part loves you too much to want you to hurt and knows you don't deserve to pay for what happened. I want to be free, Benedict. But I also want us to be free."*

He thought of the way Elysium had described their souls—teeth with roots knotted together. Pull one, and they would both go. What a bloody, painful analogy. "What do you want to do?" he asked, but he knew the answer, he felt it like it was his own and stared deep into the growing light behind her green eyes. "Okay," he agreed. "Okay."

His heart hammered in his chest, not from the fear of what they were going to do, but the very real danger of what his family was trying to accomplish back at the house right now. "Go. Save me. And I will save you."

Her smile warmed. Her arm stretched toward him with fingers out, her body already moving away. He reached out in return, the tips of their fingers close for a second before she moved away, running off into the trees and vanishing before she was far enough for the thick shadows of afternoon to swallow her.

Benedict started running, too. He couldn't disappear the way she could. He couldn't skip across stretches of land in seconds. He had to run, jumping logs and ducking branches, his boots sinking in the wet soil and making everything harder. He ran back to the house in a broad arch, coming out of the trees much farther from the driveway than where he had gone in. The long grass whipped at his already wet jeans, muscles burning and lungs sucking gulps of sticky air. He didn't go for the front of the house and the big doors. He went around the side, almost clipping his shoulder on the wall when he turned around the back.

The drizzling rain grew into another shower, wet and heavy in his lungs, leaving him panting even when he stopped at the back door. He waited there, catching his breath and listening to the mayhem of muffled voices inside. The panicked feeling of pending dread had eased back from his heart.

His family inside the house were shouting—screaming even. The walls trembled, vibrating in a low, ceaseless hum. He toed off his muddy boots, turned the knob slowly, and slipped inside under the umbrella of chaos down the dark hallways.

"Break it, Theo!" Hazel commanded, yelling over the moaning of the house. Music was playing, almost loud enough to smother them all and seeming to come from every direction.

"You'll kill him!" Elysium roared.

They were in the séance parlor.

Benedict moved from the back door into the kitchen, padding across the hardwood on bare feet. He plucked a paring knife from the stand, small and sharp. He wasn't looking to frighten or threaten. He might have taken the cleaver or the chef's knife if that were the case.

He walked down the long hall, closer and closer to the parlor.

"If her spirit is bound to Ben, it could kill him!" Elysium shouted over the music.

Benedict pressed his shoulder to the doorframe, turning just enough to see into half the parlor. Elysium was on the far side of the room, his clothing rumpled and leaning his weight onto one leg. The chair behind him had toppled over and the picture frames had been knocked from the wall. Had he been thrown? Perhaps Emmeline had done it. Or Mother.

Theodore shifted, catching Benedict's eye. His cousin had his back to him, staring at Elysium and hugging himself. He shook his head wildly. "We're going to die if we don't stop her..." he whined.

"This won't help!" Elysium yelled. That awful howl of music continued to batter eardrums, pouring out of the walls. It was too many songs at the same time, too many instruments and tempos in competition with one another, and

Benedict was certain at least one of the songs played backward, making that strange, warped sound. "Her spirit is too strong—like Mothers. It'll just set her spirit free and kill Benedict!" Elysium continued.

Benedict felt the edges of guilt creep into his heart. Elysium was still championing for his life, still trying to save his baby brother. But wasn't that what had started all of this? Mother and Uncle Vernon were ready to kill the failed Lyon all those years ago. But not Elysium. Not his brother.

"Do it!" Hazel raged. She was deeper in the room, around the corner and out of Benedict's sightlines. "They're tangled up. Killing Benedict will kill her!"

She sounded truly mad now. Emmeline was already dead, and the Lyons never used the word "kill" for a spirit. It was laughable to think on it now, that it had been a distasteful word to people who had butchered a person in their basement.

Theodore trembled but started to lift his arms from where he held them tight to his chest. That was when Benedict saw it, the big white plate he clutched in both hands.

The poltergeist seemed to have struck out at Hazel and Elysium but left Theodore untouched. Benedict understood, now that he could see the fragile talisman his cousin held—the one that could end his life.

The music grew louder, making his eardrums whistle and his skull throb. Hazel screamed in pain somewhere in the room.

A name was written on the plate, between runes he

himself had drawn a hundred times.

Emmeline Whitney Scott. He had never known her full name. But, of course, they had. They had stolen her from her life and, in their own way, thought they put her to rest at the edge of the graveyard nine years ago.

Again, Benedict imagined teeth being pulled—one tooth caught in the grip of a pair of pliers and being jerked up, ripped from the jaw and gums and dragging the other tooth with it in a bloody, mangled mess.

Elysium shouted, but the awful music drowned him out, his mouth open wide and face red, as he lunged for their cousin and the plate. He would never reach in time.

Benedict stepped through the doorway and right up behind his cousin. He had loved Theodore once, the way anyone casually loves the relations they have no reason to despise.

His right hand tightened around the handle of the paring knife, arm thrusting forward and burying the short blade into the other man's side. Benedict's chest pressed up against Theodore's back, and his free hand shot out to catch the plate just before it fell. He pulled it safely to his side and jerked the knife up. It stopped against Theodore's ribs, scraping bone. His cousin's body twitched, trying to get away with a forward lean, but Benedict walked with him. He kept Theodore's back against his chest and started pushing the blade forward, slicing his stomach open until Benedict's knife-arm was all the way around him, hugging him.

It was all without sound. He couldn't hear Theodore's

shoes scuffing the floor, couldn't hear if he screamed or gasped or begged. That would have been terrible—to hear him beg. He couldn't even hear whatever sounds the knife made against the other man's shirt, flesh, and bones.

Benedict hugged him tightly when he began to convulse, thoughtlessly digging the knife in deeper, pushing in and up. He had no idea what kind of damage he was doing, or if he should pull the knife out and try again for something more vital. Wasn't it all vital? People were fragile animals; even in the arena of mammals, they were particularly soft.

Theodore sagged, legs finally giving out rather than pedaling forward, and Benedict pulled the short blade out of him and let his cousin fall.

The rampant music in the walls stopped, his ears still ringing when he registered the *thud* of Theodore landing on the rug. His knees hit first, and then he buckled forward. His forehead smacked the ground, body slumping over.

Hazel screamed.

Benedict turned to look at her for the first time. She had propped herself against the wall. The big séance table was upside down beside her, and her leg broken, her knee crushed, and her shin bending near the middle. Had the table landed on her? Had she managed to get it off? Hazel would. She had the will to overcome her own pain. That was the point, wasn't it? The Lyons had an excess of will— too much spirit. It had allowed them to bully ghosts out of existence, and with all that will came a wealth of ego to tell them they were right to do so—not bullies, but heroes.

Tears ran in thick streaks down her cheeks, and bleary eyes fixed on her dead brother. She had lost everyone now, hadn't she? Everyone in this house anyway. Just two shitty cousins left, and no one to take her side. Not even Elysium, who was in the same sinking boat.

"This isn't you, Benny," Elysium spoke. Was he yelling, or were his ears still ringing? Somehow, he seemed loud and far away at the same time. "This isn't your anger. It's hers."

"I know. You think I don't know?" Benedict glanced down at the knife in his hand, momentarily shocked to find his arm up to his elbow covered in hot red. He trembled, eyes tearing but mouth pulling into a miserable grin. "Does the fact that it's her anger make it any less meaningful? You killed her. You murdered her. Sacrificed her, for what? For me?"

"Ben, please!" Hazel cried, croaking up the words. Her whole torso rocked, and he knew she wanted to stand or maybe even just crawl toward them. She was a doer, not the sort to sit back and let the world roll over her. But that leg wasn't going to let her move anywhere. "Smash the damn plate!"

He turned toward her, cocking a brow and holding the plate up. "This one? You want me to break this? Why? *Convince me.*" It was cruel. Was it his cruelty or Emmeline's? Did it matter?

"She's going to kill us!" Hazel burst.

Benedict laughed.

She squirmed, groping at the wall, still trying to get to her feet. "I have kids!"

His laugh died, smile dragged down. "Do you think that's a reason to spare you? To let you go home? What will happen to them, being cared for by a murderer? You didn't even like me, Hazel. Imagine what horrible things you'd do for them."

She blinked at him, and he could see all her anger bubbling under her skin, looking for a way out but still wanting to convince him. She would say anything, if only she knew the right lie to tell.

"Please," she settled on a plea.

He sighed like he had given in. And then he rubbed his bloody arm across the plate. She screamed miserably when he coated the dish in a new layer of color, painting over and smearing the runes and that name, the name of a dead girl. He made sure to rub away enough of it in those streaks of fresh blood before tossing the plate at Hazel. It broke on the floor in front of her, thick shards skittering across the hardwood. "You're welcome," he muttered.

Elysium hobbled past, and Benedict watched like a lazy wolf, following him one step out of the parlor. His brother marched a sloppy line for the front door, and Benedict waited. Somehow, he knew it was locked. He knew there would be no escape. Just as there had been no escape for her.

Elysium twisted the knob and jerked the doors against their frame. They rocked just a little, just once, before seeming to fuse together.

Elysium tried five more times before swearing and turning, pressing his back to the door and staring at Benedict. "We're your family, Benny," he rasped.

Benedict rolled the handle of the knife against his wet palm.

Emmeline was there now, standing in the foyer, watching Elysium with a thin scowl. *"I was walking home from my friend's house,"* she said softly, mesmerized by her own memories, as though they were being played for her in his tears. *"I was in a hurry. Didn't want to be late and make my mom worry... He seemed so nice when he asked for directions. He was lost—from out of town. He kept apologizing for bothering me and even promised he wasn't one of those creeps... I guess he was something else entirely. I thought he looked kinda sad. Stressed, maybe? I had no idea. There were no warning bells, no alarms going off in my head. And then it was too late. He hit me until my limbs went heavy. Until I couldn't get up. There was another man, and they put me in the trunk..."*

Elysium dropped his head back, thumping his skull against the heavy door. "She's here, isn't she?"

A tear rolled off Benedict's left eye and down his cheek. "Yes."

Hazel cried loudly in the other room, something intangible thudding around in there with her. Mother had never liked Hazel. The music started up again, blasting through the walls, but this time only in the parlor. The doors slammed shut, muting the tangle of notes and Hazel's screams.

"I never came home," Emmeline whispered bitterly, more to herself than either of them. *"My mother waited, and I never came home."*

Benedict took two steps forward. Elysium reached out to stop him, pushing at his chest in a weak effort to throw him back, but Benedict slashed at his arm with the knife, cutting through sleeve, skin, and muscle. They struggled against one another, sloppy with exhaustion, grief, and guilt on both sides. Elysium never tried to strike back at him, only tried to push him away—to grab at the hand wielding the blade and hold it back from his abdomen.

When Benedict finally shoved himself back, staggering away from the door, Elysium slid down to the floor. He panted for air, arms curling around his middle, around those seven wounds in his stomach. The knife hadn't been as big as the one they had used on Emmeline, but it would kill him—eventually.

Benedict sank back into the hall, away from the threads of gray light that saturated the front of the house, and away from the growing puddle of blood around the front door, where his brother sat.

He put the knife back in the kitchen and then went upstairs to shower.

Chapter Eighteen

Benedict woke gently, slowly, and found himself lying on his side on the bed. Emmeline mirrored him, her hand close to his, as though they might touch if only one of them would close the distance. He smiled at her first, and she smiled back cautiously. He realized then how quiet the house was. It had stopped raining outside, and there was no one moving inside but them.

He thought about how he had left his brother and cousin downstairs, knowing they were bugs in a spider's web—going nowhere.

He had showered, washing off the blood and the mud, and then laid down.

"Is it time?" he asked, though he felt it.

"*Almost,*" she said. "*You don't have to, though. You could leave.*"

Benedict rolled off the bed and stretched, just the way he did at home in their little apartment in the city. "I might be a liar, Em, but I'm not a coward."

She got up and followed him out of his bedroom and through the little sitting room.

"What should we call you?" Benedict asked. He felt better than he had since he first stepped foot into this house days ago.

"*Hm?*" Emmeline slid past while he held the door. She wore the boots, or rather, her ghostly version.

"If we were writing about you in our book of spirits, what would we call you?"

She laughed shortly and joined him in a walk down the long, dark corridor toward the stairs. *"How about, The Whispering Dead Girl?"*

He snorted. "More like, *The Shouting, Shrieking, Cackling Dead Girl…*"

She feigned offense. *"How dare you!"*

The rug at the bottom of the stairs made a soggy wet sound when he stepped on it. The hard, toxic stink of fuel hit his lungs for the second time today. Before showering, he had siphoned the fuel from the cars into the red, plastic cans in the garage and doused the first floor of the house. He paused in the foyer, considering the still shape of his brother sitting against the front doors in a puddle of blood. His legs were sprawled, and his head hung forward, chin to his chest.

Two steps and he pushed open the parlor door. He didn't step into the ruined room, furniture broken and tossed about. Theodore's body face-down on the rug where Benedict had left him and Hazel's on the far side of the room, head smashed against the edge of a table.

It didn't matter.

They didn't matter.

The big clock began to sing midnight to the house, one long chime at a time.

Benedict smiled, swinging into the dining room with Emmeline on his heels. "How about *The Midnight Ghost?*" He jumped up to sit on the table, facing the wall of family portraits.

She sat beside him, kicking her heels. *"I don't want to be called a ghost…"* she complained.

"How about, *My Midnight Lullaby* then?"

She looked at him, surprised. If she could blush, she might have.

They were seven chimes in to twelve now.

"What happens when we die?" Benedict asked, picking up the box of matches he had left on the table.

"I don't know," she confessed. *"But I'm pretty sure we'll still be together."*

He lit a match. "I hope so."

ABOUT THE AUTHOR

Cheryl Low might be a ghost haunting an apartment building in Sweden where she bakes mountains of cookies she can't eat, whispers dad jokes in the ears of her neighbors, and mixes the letters around in the mailboxes.

...Or she might be a completely corporeal hermit and no cookie in her home has ever gone uneaten.

Find out for yourself by following her on social media @cherylwlow or check out her webpage, CherylLow.com.

The answer could surprise you!

But it probably won't.

And be sure to check out
these other titles from
Grinning Skull Press

Prologue

The sailor ran toward the sound of the ocean, stumbling blindly through the midnight jungle. Mammals, birds, and insects screamed and chirped, calling out into the night as though to mask the sound of waves—working with the nightmare of this island to keep him forever lost inside a prison of foliage and teeth.

Only days ago they'd thought this island a blessing, gifted to them in the aftermath of a storm and the sinking of their ship.

They had been wrong—and now he was the only one left. The jungle had claimed the others, one by one. Blood plastered his clothes to his chest, sticking to his hands, but it wasn't his.

His boot caught on some vicious, overgrown root of the jungle floor, casting him forward onto his belly just as he broke free of the trees and vines. For a moment he didn't move to rise, panting against the coarse sand and listening to the waves. They called him, beckoning him to the only escape left.

He lifted his head, and under the bright moon, he saw the shimmering ocean, beautiful with her offer of certain death. He crawled to her, clawing and kicking at the sand in a frantic race to the foam gathering at the edge of her surf.

The ravenous jungle behind him went quiet, and that silence stabbed at his heart, bringing tears to his eyes. "It will not be me. It will not be me."

He stretched, desperate for the waves. "You will not take me."

His body jerked to a stop, fingers curling back just as the water would have reached him.

A violent breath sucked deep into his chest, burning through his lungs, his muscles, his soul—leaving nothing behind but a body sitting on the beach, smiling at the moon.

With a sigh, he stood. The waves crashed and rolled with new anger, reaching for him, always reaching. The man, no longer himself, took a step back, and then another until he disappeared into the shadows of his jungle once more.

Chapter 1

As a child, Valarie DeNola would jump right into the deep end of the pool. She wouldn't dip her toes or wade in slowly on the steps of the shallow end. She wouldn't even look into the water before leaping. She just shed her towel and her mother's hand and ran full force to the edge, jumping high and falling hard into the deep. That never changed. Not even when she traded a pool for the ocean.

* * *

To say there is no sound underwater isn't true. The press against her eardrums, the beating of her pulse, and the shifting of her suit was sound all its own—blocking out any chance of quiet. But sound was different below water than above, contained by her skull and echoing from her body.

Val held onto the bar of her cage and stared out into the deep. She loved this moment, the one when waiting became almost unbearable. Bits of fish gore fluttered through the water from the boat above. The passengers were chumming while she and the other divers waited. It wasn't difficult to find predators in these waters, and experience had taught Val that it wouldn't take long. Through goggles she watched, straining to make out moving shapes, darker blues drifting closer. The excitement clogged her throat, fingers gripping the cage as that body swam closer and closer, unable to tell size and distance until it was finally clear within sight and still so large.

Her earpiece crackled when the crew on deck saw the shark from their perch. "Incoming," Jessie said excitedly.

Val reached out to the side to grab onto Terrance's shoulder. He'd been fidgety in the cage the past few days, but he was getting better. He held onto his camera with both hands, body turning toward the viewing frame in the bars. But he didn't face it just because it offered the best view. It was where he would feel the most vulnerable, and that camera in his hands became the last barrier between himself and whatever came up from the deep. Terrance learned quickly, even if it was his first season in the water with them. Felix liked him, but no one was surprised there. Her husband could befriend a feral baboon if given some time and a bottle of tequila.

Val looked to the second shark cage dangling there in the open water, bobbing with large, black floaties breaking the surface overhead. Felix and another videographer were there to mirror them in their wetsuits and dive gear.

The shark came in close, swimming between the two cages to take a look at the boat before circling Felix. "Anyone we know?" Val asked, watching him study the massive fish. It was at least sixteen feet and female. If they didn't know her, they should. They had been coming to this spot to observe the great whites for the last four years. Val could see the bright yellow tag on the dorsal fin from where she bobbed in her own cage.

"Looks like Mimi," Felix replied in her left ear, his thick Spanish accent familiar and always comforting.

Val shifted in the cage to trade sides with Terrance, making sure he had the best shots he could get. Usually, she would have a camera herself, but with the new show they were filming, they agreed to take on more camera crew and get her into some of the shots for once.

For the past six years, it had been Felix on the screen and Val holding the camera. She used to tell him what he was looking at, what kinds of fish they were, and what was normal or abnormal about them, but Felix learned fast; she never had to tell him anything twice.

She had expected Felix to get bored with the ocean

eventually, the way he'd gotten bored with skydiving, helicopter flying, mountain climbing, and extreme camping before they met. But she had been wrong. Something about the ocean captivated him the way it did her. They could go to the same spots every year to see the same sharks, and somehow it never got old.

"We have two more, Val," Felix said over the comm system. Excitement rang in his voice, inciting it in everyone who heard him.

The cage rocked, and Val snapped her head to the side to see the large body of a male great white push past. Terrance bumped into her, and she braced his side to keep him steady while he filmed. She was sure he'd get the hang of this job—eventually.

The shark rushed up to the surface toward the boat, attacking the chum as though it might make a run for it.

The third shark rolled by in the wake of the male, swimming right by the cage to eye them. For one sickly moment, Val worried it would whip its head right through that gap of steel bars. It wouldn't fit, she was positive, but that didn't stop her stomach from lifting up into her throat when it looked back at her, seeming to hear her thoughts. When that big, black eye looked away, she noticed the pattern of scars along the head of the shark and the old scar on her pectoral fin.

"Kajsa," Val breathed. She'd named the shark after a mountain in Sweden that she had climbed with her sister after graduation. Val still had another year of schooling left at the time and no idea that it would lead her to the ocean years later, filming sharks with her husband and a team of fanatics and camera jockeys.

They'd tagged Kajsa on their first trip to this spot and took notice of her every season since. She was big, and she knew it. She liked to push the cages around. Last year she'd even gnawed one of the floaties to pieces. Felix loved her because unpredictable sharks made for thrilling footage and exciting dives. Val wasn't as enthusiastic about the big brute.

"I was wondering when we'd see her." Felix laughed over the comm, and it crackled in her ear.

Val watched the shark drift away, back down into the dark. Her heartbeat picked up the moment she lost sight of Kajsa, but by then the male had circled around and was bumping Felix's cage, giving the other cage a close encounter and Terrance some great footage.

For a few more minutes, everything went smoothly. Just enough excitement to keep everyone laughing and grinning on adrenaline. A chill ran up her spine, making her shake out her shoulders and turn her head to the side, expecting to see something stalking her in the deep. Instead, she saw Felix in his cage across the blue. Everything was a sort of slow-motion underwater. She exhaled, and bubbles rolled up toward the surface.

And then Kajsa hit her cage full force. Not from the

side, but from the bottom. Slamming hard against the gate at their feet and pushing with such force that the whole thing launched upward. The cage broke the surface, and for a horrible second, gravity was upon them, pulling Val and Terrance against the bars. The bright morning sun glared down at them before the cage tipped forward.

Val slammed against the bars of the half wall, grabbing at them to hang on when the floaties smacked against the surface of the ocean. She expected the cage to swing back down into the usual upright position, but Kajsa was still under them. Still pushing. Still thrashing.

Val couldn't hear anything when everyone started shouting over the comm system at the same time. Their voices became a tangled mess that blared through the earpiece to rival her own pulse. With that massive, toothed fish beneath, she couldn't be sure if she was even breathing. Her fingers clutched so tightly at the bars that the bones in her arms strained and shook. Her legs kicked, trying to pull up under herself for fear of popping out of the cage through the viewing hole now beneath her.

Somewhere in the flurry of sounds and panic, she heard Felix's voice shouting "babe" in that sharp tone he always said that particular pet name in. It was something he said when she was close to danger—or in this case, teeth. It wasn't creative or cute or even all that endearing, like the plethora of nicknames he'd made up for her over the years. It was the tone and the word he used when he was afraid, and it set her nerves on fire. She sucked in a breath that made her lungs ache to scream or curse.

She had forgotten Terrance entirely until his camera sunk into the blue in her line of sight. It had fallen out of the cage through the large viewing frame set in the bars. She tasted bile when Terrance sank into the deep after it.

For a sickly half-second, Val clung to the bars, leaning out that gap in the cage. She stared past the thrashing of Kajsa's tail and the glint of teeth, through the bubbles of the foaming surface at Terrance's body sinking, falling. His arms stretched to grab at the camera he'd dropped before he twisted around entirely to look up at her, up at the cage he was no longer tucked inside of, and up at the great white violently attacking the metal that was the only promise of safety. He let the camera fall, kicking weakly to keep himself from sinking farther but with nowhere to go.

Val watched another shadow of a shark roll through the darker water beneath him, circling the scene.

She let go of the bars and slipped out of the cage, diving down after Terrance, and heard Felix shouting through the earpiece. He wasn't speaking English anymore, but she recognized the Spanish as a flurry of curses and prayers all merged into one big sacrilegious plea. She kicked the cage to launch herself out and down just as Kajsa abandoned her metal prey, bumping it one last time before swimming off to circle around.

When Kajsa moved away, the curious male shark returned, teeth bared and moving right for Terrance. Val kicked harder, heart slamming in her chest as she swam toward the scene. The shark grew larger the closer it swam, and just before she reached Terrance, she saw that black eye roll back and vanish. She grabbed onto his arm and pulled hard enough that, had this been any other situation, she might have worried about his shoulder.

Terrance bumped into her, and the shark bumped into him, pushing them roughly to the side and spinning them both. Val caught a glimpse of their cage, empty and right-side up. And beyond it, she saw the second cage with Felix and the other cameraman, Gary, fighting. He was probably trying to keep Felix in the cage.

The comm system continued to crackle violently with too many voices. The captain on deck called her name repeatedly. Gary tried to give updates to the boat about what was going on while grappling with Felix. Felix cursed a lot of people and tried to get out into the open water.

Val pushed Terrance up, ahead of herself and back toward their cage. The swim felt like a sprint, her heart pounding and her muscles burning. From the corner of her eye, Val saw another shark. She twisted when it came too close, hand stretching out to push her gloved palm against the nose, above all those teeth. She locked her elbow and kept her arm straight. Shoving hard, she pushed herself to the side.

As soon as the shark passed, Val started kicking again, swimming for the cage. When she saw Terrance climbing inside, she felt a wash of relief and maybe even disbelief. They'd actually survived. It was going to be a great story. It was going to make for great footage if Gary managed to get any of it.

Val was so close to the cage. So close to this being one of those great *close calls*.

She almost didn't see Kajsa coming from underneath. Her white belly gleamed when it reached the stretches of light and gave her away in that last second.

She heard Felix shout. Not "babe" like when he was worried or afraid, but this time it was her name. Her whole name. And it sounded like the last time she would ever hear it.

Kajsa struck her from beneath, and all Val felt was the slam of the shark's weight against her. She didn't feel teeth. The brutal force of the shark's body drove her to the surface. For one horrible moment, Val was airborne but not alone. The sky shone blue, and the sun glared brightly. The water flailed through the air by Kajsa's lashing tail, droplets glimmering like stars.

The giant shark twisted in the air and came down with Val.

And then she was alone.

She couldn't move. She wasn't even sure she was breathing. She bobbed just below the surface, looking down at the deep and at Kajsa's disappearing shadow. The shark drifted deeper and deeper, farther away from Val, and all she could wonder was, why? Why would she leave when she finally had her? All those years of watching each other. All those years of Kajsa studying their cages and getting closer and closer. She finally had Val, stunned and drifting like deadwood in the sea, and she swam away.

Val slowly started sinking, drawn downward like debris. She told herself to kick, to move, to lift her head and find the boat, but she couldn't.

A cloud of red gathered around her, wispy at the edges where it faded into the blue but sickly thick all around her body. She watched that red until the sun blinded her. Her back landed on the surface of the boat, and she finally felt the weight of gravity bearing down on her. Felix pulled off her mask and held her face in his hands. His palms were so warm against her cheeks. He said that she was going to be okay over and over again. Val wanted to nod, but she couldn't. When he had to let go of her to do something else, she turned her head to the side and saw how much thicker that red looked splattering the deck.

"You're going to be okay," Felix said again, cupping

her cheek to turn her head up so that she could only see him and the sky.

Val watched him until she lost consciousness, but even when she blacked out, she could still hear the waves smacking against the sides of the boat. She still heard the waves in the hospital, and sometimes now, years later, when she closes her eyes, no matter how far inland she might be, she still hears those waves.

Chapter 2

More than three years later, and not for the first time by a long shot, Val was on another boat in the ocean. She watched the sun come up over the blue horizon rather than looking at the island behind her. They weren't far from land, but she was more than happy to stay on the boat. The sky changed colors over the sea. She'd seen it happen at least a thousand times, the dark shades of night giving way in slow folds to light through waves of pink and orange. It never got old.

The coffee cup in her right hand passed to the left, sharing warmth between palms and digits. Kajsa had taken a chunk out of her left hand, leaving Val with three fingers and a thumb but no pinky and a particularly ugly scar trailing up her forearm. Sometimes, when changing, she took a moment to bend her arm in just the right way so that the scars lined up over her hand, forearm, upper arm, and back. All those teeth, like razors through her skin, and yet somehow the shark only took a pinky. Kajsa managed to break a number of bones and tear a lot of flesh. Even after they healed, the bruises gone and the stitches removed, the scars still looked gruesome—thick, puckered flesh in pale, jagged lines twisting around her body.

She heard Julie practically skip onto deck behind her, deeply breathing the ocean air as though for the first time. Val took another drink of coffee to hide her amusement. Even when they were kids, Julie had been a morning person. Up at dawn and happy about it. Val, on the other hand, reserved all enthusiasm for after eight.

Julie bumped into her on purpose and then promptly stole the mug from her hands. She wore a blue cable knit sweater and had her brown hair in a messy bun. When they were kids, they looked nothing alike—different noses, different heights—and yet, somehow it had all evened out over the years. On more than one occasion, Julie and Valarie convinced friends that they were twins in college.

Val pushed up the sleeves of her hoodie just as the sun finally peeked over the horizon to spread out over the surface of the water. She could hear the crew stirring down below and a particularly large grumble about creamer that had to have been Julie's fiancé, Zach. They had met in the rainforests of Peru. Julie had been there with a group of other biologists to look for new species and take samples while Zach had been there as a wildlife photographer. Love at first sight, it seemed, or, as Val liked to say, *love at first bug bite*.

Julie had dragged Val into the rainforest once, and that had been enough. She'd only managed to get her along on this trip by promising that Val wouldn't have to step foot on the island. She'd even made Julie write it into her contract with the channel they were filming for just so there couldn't be any misunderstandings.

Val turned to look at her sister. The shadowy peak of Isla de los Perdidos loomed in the still-dark sky behind her. It wasn't much. A speck of land coated in thick vegetation and humming with life, relatively untouched. A handful of attempts to make settlements on it over the last five hundred years had been unsuccessful, and the locals on the mainland offered only ghost stories for explanations.

Isla de los Perdidos was abandoned. An island within eyesight of the continent it had broken away from centuries ago and yet completely uninhabited by people. The locals wouldn't even go there to show Julie and her team around. It had all just made her more excited about the idea of spending a week on it. Julie wanted to know all of its secrets, possibly discover something new, and then show the world.

She and Zach were taking two videographers, Henry and Megan, with them. Julie had worked with them in Cameroon and boasted their skills to the company.

Val got the chance to meet them the night before when they arrived at the mainland, before boarding the Charlene, a boat she had worked on before with its captain, Kevin Lochner. She was close friends with his husband, Calvin, and had worked with him dozens of times on dives for different programs. They did tropical work along reefs and beaches in Central and South America.

"Sleep well?" Val asked her sister, knowing the answer.

"Not a wink!" Julie was too excited. She was like that, too much energy for her own good sometimes—though most of the time that energy and excitement worked in her favor.

Julie spent the last eighteen months getting together this expedition and its funding. She'd worked it out so there would be three teams with camera crews to get the most material possible for the videographers, and thus the nature channel to which Julie had pitched this whole expedition. Julie, Zach, Henry, and Megan would go to the island to unravel its mysteries. Calvin, an experienced diver and cameraman, would go with Oliver Camden, a salvager, and Maeko Watanabe, a marine biologist particularly beloved by the channel, to take a look at the reef.

At least a dozen ships had sunk in these waters, and

Julie had convinced Oliver that he might find something worthwhile. Oliver was a bit of a prick but good at his job and excited to go hunting for sunken ships.

Julie gave Val back her coffee after drinking half of it and then complaining about how much sugar was in it. Val gave her a vaguely sympathetic look. She knew what she was getting when she took it.

"So, when are you setting off?" Val asked, and Julie beamed with excitement. Val took another sip of her now-cold coffee to hide the way her sister's smile infected her own mouth.

Henry and Megan, each carrying a camera and bouncing bags of lenses and supplies on their hips, were arguing about something as they made their way up from below deck. They looked almost as eager as her sister.

Julie glanced back at them before looking at Val again, and then past her shoulder to the ocean. Val didn't think her sister was looking at anything in particular until she got that look that triggered her flashbacks from their childhood. She half expected Bobby Spencer from sixth grade to be sneaking up on her with a spider.

"We're just going to get some interviews of the teams and make sure everyone is settled in before we head out for the island," Julie said, forgetting to breathe between words, and Val knew in that instant her sister was hiding something.

Val frowned because Julie looked outright guilty. Was Bobby Spencer really emerging from the ocean behind her? Val turned her head to look back over her shoulder and squinted at the small boat making its way toward them, cutting a line from the horizon. "What do you mean settled in? We're already settled," she mumbled.

Julie took her coffee again, and Val looked at her, noting that she didn't drink it this time. She just held onto it. Was she afraid she would throw it?

"Okay. So, you know how much the network loves him," Julie started in that casual tone, the diplomatic yet somehow flippant one she liked to take up when she knew she was in trouble but had no intention of apologizing.

Val stared at her for an awkward length of time before sucking a breath and realizing what her sister had done. "No," she exhaled, then turned to look at the approaching boat again. It was much worse than some shitty eleven-year-old boy and a bug. It was her ex-husband.

"He gets great ratings, and the network just loved the idea of seeing the two of you working together again. They're talking about it being the feature of next year's summer programming!" She pitched her sentences with shrill enthusiasm now. It earned her Henry's attention, the young cameraman making his way closer to discreetly film their interaction.

Val let out a groan and grabbed her coffee cup from

her sister. Julie looked worried about the tacky green porcelain, but Val didn't throw it at anyone just yet. "I need more coffee," she mumbled, and shouldered past Julie.

Her sister heaved a whine and turned to watch her retreat. "It's mostly sugar!" she shouted after her.

"Then I need more sugar!" Val called back. Megan almost bumped into her but quickly skirted to the side, looking sheepish. She could hear Julie already recovering from their interaction to tell Henry that they could get started with the crew interviews. She would go first. Julie never shied away from being the leader. It was a great quality. It's too bad she didn't shy away from stabbing people in the back either.

Val felt abruptly trapped when she reached the little kitchen below deck. She filled her cup halfway and then started heaping in spoonfuls of sugar.

Calvin came in just in time to watch the last two spoonfuls go in and raised an eyebrow. "Looking for some diabetes to go with that sulk?" he asked, taking two mugs from the cupboard, one metal and the other chipped and stained but bearing the name "Lochner" written across its front in permanent marker. He filled both mugs with black coffee and left it at that. Neither Calvin nor his husband were fans of sugar or milk in their coffee. Val remembered from the last few times she went out to sea with them. They both enjoyed giving her a hard time when it came to her sugar intake. Calvin liked things sour, and Lochner was the classic ship's captain—he only overindulged in black coffee, facial hair, and ugly sweaters.

They were an odd pair, even at sea. Calvin was clean shaven, organized, and stylish. He had a collection of vintage t-shirts and sunglasses that Val realized after their third outing together must be extensive because she never saw him in the same ones twice. His diving gear and cameras were always meticulously cared for, and he did sets of sit-ups and push-ups every morning. She'd witnessed it a number of times and seen the results in the form of hard abs and cut traps.

Calvin was fit, and he was the kind of bastard that walked around like he didn't know it. Val, of course, didn't mind because, aside from being pleasant to look at, Calvin was a smug, funny, cocky sort of person who did amazing work filming in the water.

Lochner, on the other hand, she had never once seen off his boat. Not even in the water. In fact, Val was fairly certain she had never even seen him out of a thick sweater. He was a big man with large brown eyes and a beard that was very close to being too much. He wore a knitted ski cap all of the time, but Val could vaguely remember seeing sun-bleached curls sticking out from under it once before. While Calvin could talk for hours, Lochner kept his sentences short and rare. It insured that, when he did give a command, it got attention.

She supposed they were a lot like their mugs. Different, but both on this ship, day after day, traveling the oceans like it was all home to them.

Val looked Calvin in the eye and put another spoonful of sugar in her cup before defiantly stirring it into a thick sludge.

He smiled, sunglasses clipped to the collar of today's t-shirt—vintage X-men. "Found out about the ex coming aboard, did you?"

Val frowned deeper.

Calvin shrugged and picked up his coffees. "All passengers had to be cleared with Loch," he explained his know-how and turned away from her, heading toward the narrow stairs that led above deck.

"You could have warned me." She was sure he was still smiling.

"Could have," he agreed and then disappeared, an expert at carrying multiple full cups up the stairs of a swaying ship.

Val leaned her hip into the linoleum-coated counter and took a sip of her sweet fuel. She could hear the voices above deck. Henry had caught sight of Calvin on his way up and tried to stop him for an interview, but based on the awkward way his words dropped off, Calvin hadn't stopped in his route to the wheelhouse.

She took another sip, wondering already what she was supposed to tell those cameras. The same old stuff, she guessed. Who she was, where they were, what they were there to do, and why her. Why her was a good question. She smiled and put the lip of her mug to her mouth again. The answers were always the same. It was her job to be here because she knew the ocean and the things living in it. She was also here because her sister was the one obsessed with the island and couldn't have gathered the funding for an island expedition that may turn up nothing unless she'd promised the sure bet of shark footage for the channel. Most of all, Valarie DeNola was here because she was the fool willing to get into the water every time they gave her a chance.

One of the cabin doors opened, and Oliver Camden walked out. His short coppery hair stuck out on one side, and his skin was shaded in deep tans, hinting at the shapes of shirts he wore when sunburned. Despite bedhead, he appeared bright-eyed and ready for the day. In fact, he looked like he'd been up for a while—freshly shaven and dumping an armful of maps, rulers, pens, and a tablet onto the communal table. Val frowned because she was pretty sure he wasn't going to move that shit anytime soon by the way he immediately started spreading it all out and used cups for weights at the corners of maps.

She took another deep swallow of caffeine and sugar

and watched him. He didn't look her way or say anything to acknowledge her. At least three minutes of silence stretched out between them while Val stared at his profile, trying to decide if she was being ignored or if he was just oblivious.

At last, he looked up. But not at her. Oliver swiveled around in the tight space and noticed for the first time that something was missing.

He marched three steps and pounded his fist against a narrow cabin door. "Maeko!" he shouted through the thin wood. A grumbling came from inside. "Get the fuck up, girl!" he hollered, Irish accent thick. "I'll leave you behind if you're not ready to go in an hour." His eagerness looked greedy, and he hadn't even gotten into the water yet. Val already hated the idea of him actually finding anything worthwhile but was also pretty sure he'd make for a great show. Cameras love douchebags.

Maeko Watanabe practically stumbled out of her cabin, scrubbing her face to try to convince herself she was awake.

"Coffee?" Val suggested.

Maeko scrunched her face as though offended by the idea, but shuffled closer, drawn by the gravitation of caffeine. She pushed up the long sleeves of her tight shirt and clawed fingers through her long black hair, dragging the mess back from her pale face and binding it with one of the hair ties around her wrist.

Val scooted to the side to let the shorter woman by. She fumbled for a mug, eyes still blinking a little too slowly. Val tried not to smile.

"Get me a cup," Oliver said in that casual way, completely certain one of them would do it. Val stood there long enough to see that Maeko pretended successfully not to have heard him, filling her own cup and drinking it on her way to the bathroom.

Oliver looked up from his maps when he realized he still didn't have his coffee, and for the first time that morning, his blue eyes landed on Val. She did smile then and took a sip from her cup before turning away from him. It was going to be a long week. She climbed the narrow stairs back into the rising daylight while he grumbled a curse and got his own coffee.

There's no place quite like Cofton Grange. Set in twelve-hundred acres of hills and woodland, it is a playground for the wealthy where, for the right price, every desire is made a reality.

Tonight is special; a group of hunters have bought into the most exclusive contest, the opportunity to track and kill a fantastic and terrifying creature not of this Earth. The stakes are high, each competitor determined to claim the kudos that will come from taking down their incredible prey.

But as the moon rises and the pursuit begins, each hunter is about to find out that sometimes there are fiercer things than the competition.

Tooth and Claw—The hunt is on!

"I killed my parents when I was thirteen years old."

And now, with the murder of Missy Blake twenty-two years later, it's time for Jack Greene to finish what he started.

When the co-ed's mutilated body is found, the police are clueless, but Jack knows what killed the pretty college student; he's been hunting it for years. The hunt has been going on for too long, though, and Jack wants to end it, but he can't do it alone. The local police aren't equipped to handle the monster in their midst, so Jack recruits Major Kelly Langston, and together they set out to rid the world of this murdering creature once and for all.

A lost child.

A marriage shattered beyond repair?

John Baxter doesn't think so, which is why he has planned this weekend getaway with his wife. He expected a lot of shouting, a lot of tears, but in the end, he hoped to have a stronger foundation upon which they could start rebuilding what they had once had. What he wasn't expecting was the home invasion...and the hell that awaited them beneath the rented cabin.